A big thank you to Dean Rose, Andrew Ashby, Sonia Ashby and Ben Bishop for all their help with the book.

TALES OF GRUMPTY

PART 1

CHAPTER 1: GRUMPTY THE PYGMY ELF

Deep in the hidden depths of Finhorn Forest there lived a small community of tree elves. As their name suggests, the fair-haired creatures occupied many of the trees dotted about the settlement. The dwellings were built to purposefully avoid interfering with the natural shape and curve of the trees. As such many of the houses had the tree trunks rising through the middle of the rooms.

They had no roofs, as the large branches and leaves provided adequate cover and protection. A handful of the houses were actually carved into the tree itself, whereby the elves resided in hollowed out sections of the trunk. A few of the older inhabitants lived in cabins, situated around the grassy clearing which the trees encircled.

These were newer builds that had been constructed over the years, as the elven community had grown in size and developed their resources. The cabins were of simple design with wooden walls and doors. The roofs were made from branches that were bound together with ivy and vines, and layered on top with moss and leaves for insulation. They were also raised slightly off the ground on posts to prevent instances of flooding from the nearby lake.

The clearing and the trees encircling it were a safe area. It was risky for predators to attack a whole settlement when there was easier prey to hunt in the surrounding forest. The dwarves were the only race to have invaded in the past but a peace treaty had been signed not long after, forbidding either side from launching an attack on one another.

In one of the tree houses lived Grumpty the Pygmy Elf. He had all the features you would associate with a regular elf: pointed ears, narrow eyes, a defined jawline. However, Grumpty lacked one thing that all other elves possessed, and that was height. Elves were lean, and apart from the humans were one of the tallest races in the forest. They were light-haired with pale skin, brown eyes and freckles, although there were a handful who had blue and green eyes instead.

Their outfits consisted of shirts and shorts made out of hemp, and moleskin boots and hats, both harvested from the plants around the clearing. They led simple lives such as working the land and child rearing, and although they weren't lazy, they enjoyed time spent sitting contentedly outside their huts of an evening.

Elves did shrink a little as they reached old age, but only by an inch or two. Grumpty on the other hand was more in keeping with the size of a short dwarf than a tall elf. It caused many problems for Grumpty, as he never felt truly accepted by his fellow elves. Many of the younger elves found great pleasure in teasing Grumpty, and he recalled one night in particular when he had overheard his parents arguing about him. His father had made a comment about how disappointed he was with Grumpty's height. His mother had defended him ardently, but it was too late, the damage had already been done. Grumpty felt like an outcast, living in a community where he didn't belong.

~~~

One day Grumpty was playing with some of the other elves by the village pond. It was a rare occurrence as Grumpty didn't have any friends. The only reason he had been allowed to play with them on this occasion was because it was his thirteenth birthday, and the other elves had been instructed to do so by their nagging parents. It had been going well so far. They hadn't played any pranks on him or teased him about his height. Grumpty was happy for once and wished that it could happen more often.

Unfortunately, the momentary period of bliss was suddenly shattered when Ogle, the group ringleader, dared Grumpty to go outside of the village into the forest alone. Young elves weren't allowed out of the village by themselves. There were too many dangers, such as humans and wolves. Most of the time the humans kept to themselves, not straying too far from their settlements, but occasionally a few would venture out into the woods on hunting expeditions. They wouldn't dare attack the whole village, but a solitary young elf walking all alone would be an easy target.

Being the ringleader of the elven gang Ogle always had the final say. The other elves weren't normally so bad when he wasn't around, as they usually grew bored teasing Grumpty and left him to his own devices. But when Ogle was there, he brought out the worst in them, suggesting wicked schemes to enact on the unfortunate small elf. Grumpty considered arguing even if suffering a beating. Ogle and his gang were scary but Grumpty feared the forest insurmountably more.

There were rumours that a beast lurked there far more cruel and evil than humans. One of the elders actually claimed to have seen the creature in his youth, before fleeing back to the village in terror. He had only glimpsed the beast for a moment but according to the elf it had had a pair of large horns and thick black fur. However, Grumpty couldn't help feeling that the older elves had said this just to stop the younger elves from straying too far.

Grumpty's train of thought was suddenly interrupted when the impatient Ogle shoved him hard in the chest. Grumpty stumbled back, tripping over a protruding root and flew head-first into the pond with a loud splash. The other elves sniggered as Grumpty emerged a few seconds later, spluttering and coughing.

Ogle led them away leaving Grumpty to flop back onto dry land. He was in a foul mood, not helped by the fact that his tunic and shorts were soaked right through. Grumpty fished his acorn hat out of the pond and marched briskly through the village, his moleskin boots squelching loudly.

He received many puzzled and curious glances as he stormed past. Ogle and his gang were loitering at the edge of the village, most probably hatching another evil scheme. They turned upon seeing Grumpty approaching and burst into laughter, pointing and clapping. Much to their astonishment Grumpty ignored them and headed for the path leading away from the village.

~~~

A short while later Grumpty found himself wandering between the tall trees of Finhorn Forest. He glanced over his shoulder and felt frightened all of a sudden. The village was no longer in sight. The realization that he was now on his own began to slowly dawn on him. Grumpty took stock of how dark it was becoming and shivered, his damp clothes making his nose run.

He had been walking for some time now, his determination to put as much distance between himself and the elves pushing him on. But as he had got further and further away and the light had gradually faded, Grumpty's feeling of hot anger had turned to anxiety and growing fear.

At the start of the walk the forest had looked pretty and idyllic in the daylight, with the sun dappling through the leaves. But now in the dusk everything looked cold and formidable. Every now and then a branch or twig would snap from somewhere in the trees, and once or twice he had spotted dark shapes moving around in the shadows. The birds that had previously been singing so pleasantly were now quiet, and the only calls Grumpty could hear were high pitched shrieks that sent a shiver down his spine.

A fallen log on the path ahead forced him to stop and he took the opportunity to rest for a minute. The log was high, but he managed to scramble up it and perch on the edge. His short legs dangled over the side, shaking slightly from a combined lack of warmth and nerves. An owl hooted in the trees above, causing him to glance around nervously. He couldn't see any sign of the creature but he had the uneasy feeling that it was out there some-where, watching him from the shadows.

The tall, dark trees were imposing and Grumpty couldn't shake the feeling that the towering forest had crept closer when he wasn't looking. There was a sudden flapping noise from behind him and spinning round he let out a loud yelp. A huge owl materi-alized out of the darkness and scooped him up with its large, razor sharp talons.

CHAPTER 2: GRUMPTY'S WELCOME HOME

Ogle sat in his bedroom, throwing a large pinecone against the wall. It wasn't common practice to keep them as mementos, as elves weren't materialistic by nature. However, Ogle had hung on to it as it had a nice weight and shape that made it ideal for throwing and catching.

Nearly a year had passed since Grumpty had walked out of the village, never to return. Not long after, Ogle had sworn his friends to secrecy, not wanting the truth to come out that he had dared Grumpty to leave the village in the first place. He did feel a level of guilt about what he had done but not enough to come clean and confess to his or Grumpty's parents.

A party of brave elves had ventured out into the forest to look for Grumpty but after three days spent searching the nearby woods, they had turned up nothing. So, in the end they had been forced to abandon the task. They had not wanted to lose further elves while in the process.

Ogle was not having a good day. All his friends had gone down to Lughorn Lake as part of their school trip. The lake was located at the very edge of the village and younger elves were only ever allowed there accompanied by an adult. Ogle wasn't allowed to go on account of having been grounded, due to being caught stealing acorns from Father Mugleaf's orchard.

Ogle let loose some of his aggression on the pinecone and

groaned as it missed the wall and sailed out of the window. Reluctantly he pushed himself off the bed and went to have a look. Peering over the window ledge, he scanned the ground for the fallen pinecone. All of a sudden a large shadow emerged over the patch of grass, revealing the outline of two great wings.

Ogle shrank back inside terror stricken. But instead of a mighty winged predator, Ogle was astounded to discover the small form of Grumpty soar past, two makeshift wings attached to his shoulders. Ogle watched on amazed as Grumpty slowly descended and landed on top of a large mossy stone.

The night Grumpty had been snatched up by the owl, he had been taken back to the creature's nest. The Mother Owl's plan was to feed her young owlets with the lost elf, as she did with all small creatures she found on her nightly hunts. However, upon hearing the short elf's heart wrenching story she had taken pity on Grumpty.

She took the young elf, literally, under her wing and spent the next year raising him as one of her own. The Mother Owl had even helped Grumpty fashion a pair of makeshift wings.

They were constructed using a skeleton of branches, layered with leaves. It wasn't advanced enough to manipulate the frame to allow flapping. However, if taken high enough Grumpty was able to glide above the trees for a while.

And that is exactly what had happened. With the aid of Mother Owl and some of the younger owls, Grumpty had been escorted high into the air. There he had been let free by the owls and had glided back to the village where he had grown up.

~~~

The news of Grumpty's return had spread like wildfire throughout the village. As more elves learnt of the alarming news, a crowd had begun to gather around the large mossy stone upon which Grumpty proudly stood upon. He cut quite the impressive figure with his majestic looking wings, and as more elves began to approach the stone, questions were directed his way.

Chores and jobs were suddenly forgotten about and the young elves were even allowed out of afternoon school lessons for the special occasion. For the first time in Grumpty's life he felt truly respected by the elven community.

Whispers and hushed voices rippled around the converging group as they gazed up at him with excited and startled expressions. The only elf not in attendance was Father Mugleaf, who was cowering behind the oak altar in the village church.

Mugleaf had been tending to his acorn trees in the churchyard when he had spotted a mysterious black shape high in the sky. Due to the bright midday sun all he had managed to make out was a large shadow with giant wings. Fearing it to be a demon sent from the underworld to punish the elves for their sinful ways, he had dropped his watering can and hurriedly scuttled inside the church.

Unfortunately, no one had been able to reach Mugleaf to inform him of the creature's identity. He had bolted shut the church doors hoping that the holy place of worship might protect him from the winged terror. When silence had descended Mugleaf had ventured a peek over the altar but had quickly ducked down when he heard, what he believed to be, the sound of elves screaming in terror. But he had been mistaken.

The elves had not been crying out in fear but instead cheering in delight as Grumpty had proudly displayed his impressive wings. No one more so than Barkle the Inventor, who upon seeing the majestic form of Grumpty atop the stone had shouldered and barged his way to the front of the crowd, eager to understand the mechanics of the custom-made wings.

As Grumpty twirled on the spot, allowing the cool breeze to ruffle his leafy wings he grinned from ear to ear at his captivated audience. His smile faltered slightly when he became aware of the absense of his mother and father. The elves were taking him seriously now. Not just a pint-sized elf that they could make fun of anymore. Grumpty suddenly felt a tremendous amount of power and influence over the small assembly and he was going to enjoy it as much as possible. Barkle jumped up and down like an excited puppy as he scrutinized the elaborate wings.

~ ~ ~

Later that night there was much rejoicing at Grumpty's return and a great feast was put on to mark the occasion. The only elves who were not in attendance were his parents, who according to Barkle, had disappeared when they had ventured into the forest in search of their son not long after he had gone missing. He was deeply saddened by the news that they hadn't returned, especially in regards to his mother, but he decided to put the matter to the back of his mind for the time being.

A large tent had been erected in the centre of the village, its design of orange, green and warm brown colours further enhancing the pretty glade surrounding it. Grumpty couldn't seem to get a moment's rest.

If it wasn't Barkle pestering him about the design of his wings, then it was the younglings asking him to tell them stories of his grand adventures beyond the forest wall. Grumpty had grown tired of Barkle and his continual stream of questions, but he took great delight in recalling his adventures to the little ones.

As the night of festivities carried on and the acorn wine began to flow more freely, Grumpty felt a fuzzy warm feeling flow through his body. It was his first-time drinking wine and he had been surprised to learn that he quite liked the taste of it. He was only allowed one cup and it had been watered down, but it still made Grumpty feel that tiny bit more mature. The other elves adored him, and since his arrival he had been plied with heaps of gifts and mountains of food. He had lapped it all up, filling his gut to the point of bursting.

The only dampener on the evening had been when Ogle had arrived at the party. The hiccup was soon remedied when Ogle had tried and failed miserably to embarrass and upstage Grumpty, by holding two leaves in his hands and flapping his arms, trying to imitate the pygmy elf. Ogle had been heckled and booed by the revelling elves until eventually he had relented and retreated to a corner of the party tent, to sulk in the shadows.

Grumpty glanced over at where Ogle sat and was delighted to see how miserable he looked. Ogle caught his eye and Grumpty gave him a huge grin and raised his cup of acorn wine to him. Furious and red faced Ogle stormed out of the party, leaving Grumpty to giggle with the younglings.

~~~

The next day Grumpty was roughly awoken by a series of loud bangs on the side of his treehouse. He groaned, feeling uncomfortable from too much rich food from the night before. He begrudgingly got up and pulled back the entrance flap, wincing slightly as he was hit in the face by the bright morning light. When he had recovered from the shock of the outside world, he was surprised to find Ogle waiting on the veranda outside.

~~~

A small cluster of elves stood huddled around the mossy stone; their expressions grim. Grumpty sat on top of the stone, deep in thought. He had chosen this spot as the stone was often used as a platform for village meetings and announcements. During the night Ogle's mother had gone missing. Ogle had presumed she had gone to the lake to get fish but after three hours there still hadn't been any sign of her.

Nut, the village elder and continual bearer of bad news believed that a young wolf might have kidnapped her, as part of their initiation into wolf adulthood. As much as no one in the village wanted to face that grim prospect, the truth was that it was a regular occurrence.

Azral the Trader had learnt from his travels to the neighbouring villages, that there had been a spree of elfnap related incidents in the last couple of months. Elves were supposed to travel in small groups to lower the chances of attack, so either Ogle's mother had forgotten to follow the advice or chosen to dismiss it. Ogle had already appealed to the elves to help him rescue his mother and although they felt sorry for him, they were reluctant to undertake such a perilous mission.

Grumpty sighed and regarded Ogle quietly for a moment. Here in front of him stood the elf who used to torment him on a daily basis, who had single handily ruined his childhood years. And yet Grumpty couldn't help but feel sorry for the distraught elf. Menace or not, no elf should be separated from their mother.

So, bearing this in mind Grumpty climbed slowly to his feet and announced that he, Grumpty, would go with Ogle in search of his mother. Ogle was so grateful for the kind gesture that he threw himself on the ground and begged for forgiveness for his past sins.

After much discussion and deliberation, it was decided that a small team from the village would accompany Grumpty and Ogle on their journey into the forest. Azral and Nut would provide navigation, as they were the two elves with the most extensive knowledge of the forest itself. Barkle would also tag along, as his skills as an inventor would come in useful when setting up a camp.

Lastly, Father Mugleaf had joined up, as he felt guilty at his action of barricading himself in his church and leaving the village to its fate when Grumpty had arrived. So, the six elves set off from the village and Grumpty found himself travelling alongside his former nemesis.

CHAPTER 3:
HONEYGLADE TOWN

Grumpty woke early and tiptoed over the sleeping bodies of his fellow travellers in the half-light filtering between the large tree roots. They had set up camp under a broad tree, as it provided good cover from predators, while also shielding them from any adverse weather. Grumpty made his way silently up the steep incline of damp soil, rising to one of the gaps in the gnarled cluster of roots and peered outside.

It was an immensely bright day and Grumpty had to grip on to the huge trunk of the tree, to stop himself toppling backwards from the glare. Once his eyes had adjusted, he squeezed through the gap and jumped down onto the soft grass outside. Up ahead was a small beach of pebbles stretching out until it gradually disappeared into a wide and sweeping river.

As Grumpty made his way over to the riverside, he took stock of the glorious morning about him. He wandered across the floor of pebbles; the hardened soles of his feet accustomed to rough terrain. At the water's edge he paused and let out a loud yawn. His eyes were heavily bloodshot and underset by dark bags. Grumpty was grumpy. Deep wrinkles were etched across his forehead, pulled together in a moody frown. Three days had passed since their quest had begun, and so far Grumpty hadn't had a single decent night's sleep. The first night he had had to endure the sobs and wails of Ogle caught in the throes of recurring nightmares about his stolen mother.

The second night he had been awoken by an owl's hoot and

had stumbled outside to find Mother Owl and two of the older owlets. They had tracked Grumpty and his companions' progress, worried that things had turned sour and Grumpty had been kidnapped by the other elves. She had been about to send in one of the owlets to retrieve him when Grumpty had staggered out into the moonlight.

After much discussion, Grumpty had managed to explain the real reason he was travelling with a group of elves from the village. Mother Owl hadn't been impressed, finding it difficult to digest the fact that Grumpty was working alongside those that had cast him out. However, Grumpty was determined to see the task through and Mother Owl accepted the fact that there was no changing his mind.

They had left soon after, telling Grumpty to take care and offering assistance by scouting out the forest ahead for signs of wolves in the nearby area. The predators tended to travel in packs and it was likely that if Ogle's mother had been stolen by a young wolf it would have taken her back to a communal den. The thought of coming face to face with one wolf was terrifying enough but a whole pack didn't bear thinking about. The group had tried to keep in good spirits but Grumpty could tell they were all just as scared as he was.

Last night hadn't been any better. Grumpty had tossed and turned all night, plagued with troubled thoughts. He had returned to the village a new elf and despite the bad memories that frequented the village, he had discovered how much he enjoyed the company of other elves. It worried Grumpty because he also felt a responsibility to the owls.

They were his true family who had treated him with respect and compassion, and taught him a great many wise and insightful things. Thus, Grumpty felt torn. His head was a foggy blur, unable to make a clear decision, not helped by the lack of sleep. He sighed and rubbed his tired eyes. It was going to be a long day.

~~~

The others rose a few hours later and found Grumpty asleep on the grass, snoring loudly. They began packing up their provisions and equipment, while Ogle, who was unlucky enough to pull the short straw. was tasked with the challenge of waking the slumbering elf. Azral and Nut were in the middle of a heated argument about which way to go next when a loud yelp interrupted their bickering.

Much to their amusement, they spotted a terrified Ogle tearing across the pebbled beach, pursued by an irate Grumpty brandishing a large stick. Ogle had rather stupidly poured cold river water over the sleeping Grumpty,after failing several times to wake him gently. Both Azral and Nut burst into laughter at the peculiar display and their disagreement was soon forgotten.

Barkle, who was sitting on a log and pondering over a sketch he had made of Grumpty's wings joined in too and soon the forest was filled with elvish laughter. Mugleaf on the other hand did not look impressed and watched the chaos from the shadow of the tree with an air of distaste, his arms folded across his chest.

~~~

A few hours later and the small company of elves were making their way down river, headed for HoneyGlade Town. HoneyGlade was one of the biggest settlements in Finhorn Forest and attracted a great variety of visitors all year round. Originally set up by the goblins, it had begun life as a small self-contained community.

However, goblins, being greedy and business minded, had soon expanded and developed the town, luring other creatures in with the promise of cheap entertainment and otherwise hard to acquire black-market goods. Trolls and ogres were regular visitors, as they were keen traders and hagglers. In more recent years Tree Pixies had also begun to appear more regularly, as they had a reputation for gambling and HoneyGlade scratched that itch for them.

According to Azral, HoneyGlade was the last place to suffer a wolf attack. Just under a month ago, a goblin had gone missing walking home late at night and soon after paw prints had been discovered at the edge of town. Their plan was to question one of Azral's many known contacts at the HoneyGlade tavern. Grumpty, Ogle and Barkle were keen to pursue the lead, as they had walked many miles already with only the occasional paw print to keep them on track.

Nut on the other hand, bitterly opposed the idea. Despite the friendly name HoneyGlade Town was an unruly and lawless place. One had to keep an eye out around the many backstreets and side roads, as muggings and violence were a common occurrence. Nut had experienced it first-hand when he had visited the town in his early teens. A gang of street trolls had cornered him in an alley, roughed him up and stolen his beloved engraved belt that had been a gift from his late father.

The elf had returned home crestfallen and had been left with a bitter taste in his mouth for the town of HoneyGlade. Azral explained that no harm would befall them for two reasons. Azral was well known around town and relied upon for his wares and services. And secondly, a lot had changed since Nut's youth. Nut was still not convinced but was left with no choice as the other elves decided they were going there anyway, whether he liked it or not.

~~~

HoneyGlade was a shock to the system for Grumpty, Ogle and Mugleaf as they made their way down the heaving cobbled high street. All manner of creatures fought for space in the bustling throng of bodies, from Mountain Trolls to Cave Dwarves. Even a few Tree Pixies whizzed overhead. Azral, Barkle and Nut, who were more experienced in dealing with crowds, tucked in their heads and stuck out their elbows.

Grumpty didn't realise why at first, but soon understood when a lumbering River Ogre barged past him, nearly sending Grumpty spinning into a nearby market stall. Azral, Barkle and Nut were making speedy progress. Apologising profusely to the stall owner Grumpty grabbed hold of a horrified Mugleaf and a dazed Ogle, and ducked and weaved his way after the others.

~~~

The dark, near empty tavern was a welcome relief for the six elves and they collapsed onto some stools around the nearest table. Grumpty was still reeling from the intensity of the outside world. He had never seen such a variety of creatures in one place. Mugleaf was positively pale from the ordeal and clutched the edge of the table with tight fingers.

Grumpty glanced around the dim interior of the tavern. A few tables were occupied with an assortment of mean looking individuals. One of them, a large Rock Troll, gnashed his granite teeth together upon catching sight of Grumpty's curious expression. Grumpty looked away, trying not to make further eye contact with the Rock Troll.

At the back of the tavern, hidden in the semi darkness of one of the booths sat a shadowy figure, his hand clasped around a tall tankard of ale. Grumpty couldn't make out the figure's face, but he had the uneasy feeling that the stranger was watching him. Azral plonked six tankards down on the table in front of them and without a word moved over to the mysterious figure.

As they were still minors, Grumpty and Ogle only had water in their tankards but Nut let them both try a sip of the cloudy ale he was sipping from. As they finished their round, Azral returned to their table and informed the group that there was a wolf den not three days walk from HoneyGlade.

Azral's contact had advised that if they wanted any chance of finding Ogle's mother then the den would be their best bet. The news gave the group renewed hope, as it was the first shred of solid evidence they had come across in days.

Ogle's only concern was that another three days walk might not be quick enough, as he was already growing increasingly worried about his mother's safety. In the end it was agreed that Barkle and Azral would search the town for someone willing to take them downstream in a boat. By river they would reach the wolf den in a day and a half at the most. In the meantime, the rest of the group would gather supplies and sort out accommodation for the evening.

~~~

The next morning the group rose early and made their way down to the docks. Azral and Barkle had managed to persuade a local fisherman by the name of Gargol to ferry them, at a price, as far as Sticklewood, a cluster of mud huts and dwellings a few hours walk from the wolf den. Gargol was a narrow eyed, skittish looking Hobgoblin and Grumpty wasn't too keen on sharing a boat with him. There was something untrustworthy about the creature's furtive glances, but they had no choice. Gargol was the only fisherman willing to ferry them out of HoneyGlade straightaway, and the company of elves were eager to leave the hostile town as soon as possible.

The elves had tried to travel as light as possible but they still carried a knapsack of provisions each and Grumpty had also brought his makeshift wings along. Once everyone and everything was on board, they cast off and began to drift slowly away from the HoneyGlade docks.

CHAPTER 4:
STICKLEWOOD HUTS

Ogle leant over the portside of the boat, heaving and wretching in fits and starts. He stumbled back across the deck a few moments later, pale faced, his legs wobbling dangerously underneath him. Barkle grabbed hold of his arm to try and steady him, but Ogle shrugged him off and leant over the siderail once more, attacked by another wave of nausea. Gargol stood at the small vessel's rudder sneering snidely at Ogle's sorry state.

Elves weren't good at being on water. It was all to do with their connection to the earth. From a young age they were taught to listen and use the ground beneath their feet, to navigate their environments. As elves grew older and learnt more about the landscape around them, they became more in tune with it.

By age seven Grumpty was able to jump between trees with his eyes closed, his feet tracing the grooves and contours of the branches, his ears picking up the sway and flutter of the leaves in the breeze. The only downside to the amazing ability was that it meant that any other surface, such as water, posed a serious problem for the pointy eared creatures.

Grumpty wasn't as bad as the other elves, due to his time spent in the company of the owls. Learning to traverse the currents of the air had helped him get used to different environments. Still, it wasn't plain sailing by any means and it was a struggle to keep his breakfast down.

They had been sailing for half a day so far, navigating a series of narrow rivers and streams that twisted and snaked their way through the deep woods. So far Gargol had spent the majority of the journey laughing at the sick elves, picking his nose, spitting and passing wind crudely. It hadn't particularity bothered the elves, as it was common knowledge that hobgoblins were vile and rude creatures.

The only issue was that Grumpty had an uneasy feeling brewing in the pit of his stomach. Who was to say that once the elves arrived, Gargol wouldn't run off and inform the wolves of their arrival? They had paid a fair price for the journey downstream but according to Azral, it was common knowledge that wolves paid well for information about possible prey.

So Grumpty wasn't unfounded in his concerns, and bearing this in mind, he took the other elves below decks to one of the cabins to discuss it with them, out of earshot of Gargol. He was pleased to discover that he was not alone in his concerns. Azral, Nut and Barkle were also sceptical about Gargol's allegiance. Ogle would have probably been too if he hadn't been focusing all his thoughts on not throwing up.

Mugleaf on the other hand seemed unconcerned by the topic of discussion and was more interested in a large bark bound journal, which he scribbled in fastidiously. Together they formed a plan in the eventuality that Gargol might attempt to betray them.

~~~

Just when Ogle thought he could endure no more of the unsettling journey, the first mud hut came into view. This marked their arrival at Sticklewood and as the boat passed the hut and rounded a curve in the river, more huts appeared on the riverbanks either side of them. There was a surprising lack of activity to the place and the huts sat still and silent.

Grumpty wondered where all the inhabitants were, as there were no signs of anybody on the land. He looked for a campfire or signs of life in and around the dormant huts, but no such luck. As the boat slowed and pulled alongisde a deserted rotting, wooden jetty, rain began to fall lightly from the sky. Mugleaf, who had re-

25

mained silent during the voyage, turned his attention away from his scribbling and glanced up at the overcast sky and commented on how it was a bad omen.

The other elves laughed at this remark, putting it down to Mugleaf's tendencies to be over dramatic. For once Grumpty didn't join in and as he stepped off the boat onto the rickety jetty, a tight knot of anxiety began to grow inside him. This was as far as Gargol could take them by boat as the wolf den was a few hours walk inland. Once the provisions had been offloaded and Gargol had been paid the remaining half of his money, he hopped back onto his boat and continued downstream, leaving the small group of elves at the end of the jetty.

The rain was beginning to fall harder now and Nut and Barkle were keen to get inside, away from the cold. The elves navigated their way along the jetty, being careful to avoid the missing and broken slats. At the end of the jetty Mugleaf froze and refused to go any further. Azral tried to lead him away by the hand, but Mugleaf shook him off. His eyes were full of fear and he stuttered through chattering teeth that the place was cursed.

The other elves didn't laugh this time. It wasn't one of Mugleaf's usual over dramatic speeches. He truly believed in what he had said. There was no way of knowing, as none of the elves had visited the place before and Grumpty could only assume Mugleaf had said it because he was unsettled by the absence of life. Through careful coaxing, Nut eventually managed to guide Mugleaf off of the jetty and the elves were able to continue towards the abandoned huts.

It was strangely quiet, as they trudged their way between the run-down dwellings. There seemed to be a stillness that hung heavy in the air. No birds sang in the trees. No creatures stirred on the ground. It was as if the wildlife chose to avoid the area entirely. Even the flowers and grass had withered and died. The elves explored some of the huts and were surprised to find some of the tables laden with dinnerware and rotting food.

It was as if the inhabitants had simply upped and disappeared. Mugleaf refused to enter any of the dwellings until the elves were able to find a hut without a set table, and even then, it took a great deal of gentle guidance to even get him over the threshold.

By the time the elves were finally settled and had scraped together a basic, rather bland supper of stale bread, cheese and berries, they made a small fire to help dry them out. They were all in low spirits. Azral was in a particularly foul mood and kept shooting daggers at Mugleaf, who he felt was the cause for his rain soaked garments. Grumpty sat silently in one corner, entranced by the flicker and crackle of the fire.

~ ~ ~

The large, snowy white Wolf King stood on the grassy verge of the river; his piercingly sharp eyes fixated on the Sticklewood Huts, that stood on the far side of the water. Behind him a company of young, lean looking grey wolves waited patiently.

A haggard looking wolf with a jet-black coat and a large scar running through one eye stood to the Wolf King's right, his jaw dripping with frothy saliva. The Wolf King arched his neck back and let out a loud howl. The accompanying wolves joined in, their harrowing howls slicing through the night air.

CHAPTER 5: THE CLEARING

The Wolf King glanced at his second in command and motioned towards the dilapidated huts across the river. The wolves were situated a little further upstream from the jetty, where the river was slightly narrower. The haggard looking lieutenant snarled, barked viciously and set off towards the edge of the bank.

As he got closer to the water the Haggard Wolf began to pick up more speed, his muscled legs pounding the grassy turf. The agile beast let out a deep growl and sprung from the bank's lip, propelling himself through the air. The Wolf King watched pleased, as his second in command cleared the water and landed in a half slide on the other side of the bank, spraying up dirt and grass about him.

Inspired by the Haggard Wolf's success the remaining grey wolves soon followed, leaping over the rushing river to the far bank. One of the youngest wolves in the pack had the unlucky misfortune of misjudging the gap and plunged into the icy waters with a loud yelp. The Wolf King watched, his face devoid of emotion, as the young greyback kicked and fought against the rushing current.

Eventually it was too much for the poor creature and he was pulled under by the fast flow of water. A few of the grey wolves howled, pain stricken by the loss of their younger brother. The Wolf King raised his nose into the air and sniffed. The smell of elves lay heavy on the air and inhaling the aromas deep into his nostrils, he darted forwards with alarming speed and soared over the water.

~~~

Angered at the death of one of their own, the wolves tore through Sticklewood, wreaking havoc inside the huts. As the grey-backs systematically searched each hut, the Wolf King and his lieutenant paced between the dwellings, tracking the scent of the elusive elves.

Eventually, the scent led them to one of the huts at the far end of the village. The Haggard Wolf appealed to his leader to go scout it out and the Wolf King nodded, approving his eager request. The Haggard Wolf rushed forwards and dived headfirst through the hut window. He landed heavily, destroying the small, weakly built dinner table.

Wood flew into the air around him as he destroyed more of the furniture, sniffing around for the company of elves. They were no-where to be seen. One of the small creature's moleskin coats was draped over a chair, pushed up against the wall. The Haggard Wolf moved over to it, his blood boiling as he began to realize that it was the source of the scent. There was a slight snap as he stepped onto a rug. He looked down puzzled and a moment later there was a louder snap and the ornate rug gave way under his feet.

Upon hearing the Haggard's Wolf cry, the Wolf King moved cautiously towards the open hut door. Splintered bits of wood lay scattered around the dwelling and there was a large hole in one corner of the room. The Wolf King moved over to it and peered inside.

The Haggard Wolf lay at the bottom of a deep pit, tangled up in the living room rug. He was snarling and thrashing about angrily. The Wolf King glanced up and caught sight of the moleskin coat. He snarled viciously and grabbing the coat between his teeth, pro-ceeded to tear it into a thousand pieces.

~~~

Mother Owl and Azral sat on the end of a long branch, high up in a tall Birch. From their position they had a clear view of Sticklewood and watched intrigued, as the company of wolves darted frantically in and out of the huts. The owls had been keeping an eye on the elves throughout their journey, or more specifically Mother Owl had been keeping an eye on Grumpty.

When she had seen the company of wolves converging on Sticklewood, she had sent in her owls to fly the elves to freedom. At the end of the day it was the elves' quest to complete not the owls, but they couldn't sit back and see them savaged by the wolf pack.

~~~

Grumpty glided over the tall treetops, the air currents propelling him through the sky. Five owls accompanied him, each clutching a small elf in their large talons. Grumpty dipped and felt the high tree top leaves brush his legs. He started to grow worried at his closeness to the trees and glanced to one of the owls for assistance. However, as the owl swooped down to aid him, the trees petered out and large meadows and fields came into view.

Grumpty directed his wings at the ground below and slowly began to descend towards one of the overgrown meadows. Seeing his change in direction, the party of owls copied his example and gradually flew downwards. Grumpty landed in the meadow at a run, which turned into a jog and then eventually he was able to come to a stop. The owls landed more gracefully, gently resting the queasy elves amongst the wild flowers.

Being the eldest two Nut and Mugleaf looked the palest. Grumpty was the only elf that seemed to be unaffected by the journey. He wrapped his arms around Mother Owl's feathery neck, hugging her tightly. She responded by ruffling his light hair fondly with one of her feathery wings.

Once the elves had regained their sense of balance, the owls bid them farewell and departed. It was late evening and the sun was just a thin sliver of orange above the horizon. Noticing the darkening sky, Grumpty roused the seated elves much to their displeasure, and set off for the line of trees at the far end of the meadow.

~~~

Half an hour later, the elves came to a halt at the edge of a wide clearing, deep in the heart of the woods. Peering through the thin screen of bushes Grumpty could make out the form of several sleeping wolves, arranged in a circle. In the centre of the circle sat Ogle's mother looking absolutely petrified. Instinctively, Ogle went to move forwards but Grumpty placed a hand gently on his chest.

Ogle questioned his action and Grumpty nodded back to the clearing. A wolf was emerging through the trees on the other side of the clearing, slowly approaching the circle. Their hearts sank as the sentry began to casually stroll around the sleeping wolves. They were going to have to come up with a plan if they wanted any chance of rescuing Ogle's mother without being seen.

~~~

The wolf guard paced back and forth around the encampment, carrying out her sentry duties. A movement in the trees ahead made her stop and her eyes narrowed, trying to discern the mysterious presence. A branch snapped somewhere behind the bushes and the wolf guard snarled. She pondered whether to investigate or not.

Her job as wolf guard was to stick to her route and guard the prisoner, but a part of her wanted to scout out the threat and eliminate it. She could have woken one of the others but wolves were deep sleepers and irritable when disturbed. By the time she managed to rouse a fellow wolf, the bush dweller would have had time to slip away.

As she was considering her predicament, a flash of red materialized amongst the foliage and throwing caution to the wind the wolf guard darted into the trees after it. Taking a window of opportunity, Grumpty and Ogle tiptoed carefully into the clearing.

Ogle's mother spotted the two elves and was about to emit a cry of surprise before Ogle raised a finger to his lips, willing her into silence. Trying to be as quiet as possible Grumpty and Ogle stepped carefully over the snoring wolves and crept at a painstakingly slow rate, towards Ogle's mother.

The wolf guard raced further through the trees, ignoring the leaves and branches that whipped against her face. The red blur was drawing ever closer and she pushed on harder, eager to unearth its mystery. A fallen log lay ahead and she jumped over it gracefully. The red blur was close now, just behind the next clump of bushes.

The wolf guard charged through it and slid to a halt, her claws digging into the soft soil beneath her. Hanging from a tree branch in front of her was a small red elven hat. Nut's hat to be precise. The wolf guard gnashed her teeth together menacingly and she leapt up to the branch, wrenched the hat to the ground and began tearing it to pieces.

When the hat lay in tatters and the wolf guard had vented her frustration, she sniffed the remains for Nut's scent. She grinned devilishly. It was still fresh. The elf was nearby.

Grumpty and Ogle were making good progress and the pair quickened their steps, desperate to reach Ogle's petrified mother before any of the sleeping beasts stirred from their slumber. There was a moment of panic when a wolf moved beneath Grumpty as he was in the middle of stepping over him. Luckily the wolf rolled over and carried on sleeping. Grumpty let out a sigh of relief and pressed on cautiously.

Eventually, they made it to the centre and Ogle embraced his mother in a tight hug. The three elves were just about to make their way back when they heard rustling and movement in the foliage, close by.

Grumpty felt a deep fear rise within him as the Wolf King and the company of grey wolves emerged through the trees. Ogle's mother let out a little squeak and clung on to her son's arm. The

Wolf King paused at the edge of the clearing and glared at the three tiny elves, his eyes burning with a fiery intensity.

CHAPTER 6: THE ELEMENT OF SURPRISE

Ogle's legs trembled nervously in his ankle high moleskin boots, as the Wolf King began to pad slowly towards them. Grumpty glanced around anxiously at the still, sleeping bodies of the surrounding wolves. There was no escape. If they turned and ran the entire gang of wolves would be alerted and they would certainly be finished, acorn hats and all.

So, the three elves remained rooted to the spot as the great white wolf approached the outer ring of sleeping wolves. Ogle gulped loudly, his eyes darting towards Grumpty expectantly. Grumpty looked to the ground, a downcast expression on his face. Why did everyone expect him to know what to do?

The Wolf King paused in front of the first sleeping wolf and gazed down at the resting creature. He shifted his gaze to the stationary elves and slowly raised a paw above the snoring wolf. Grumpty felt the air trap in his throat as the Wolf King lifted his leg, preparing to strike. Ogle hugged his mother in a tight embrace, readying himself for the attack to come. The Haggard Wolf stood a few yards behind his master, tensing himself excitely.

Grumpty's heart raced beneath his ribcage and unable to watch, he closed his eyes. He could feel the blood pumping in his ears and the tips of his fingers quivering, coated in a thin layer of sweat. Grumpty inhaled deeply, waiting, listening for the yelp of the sleeping wolf.

The yelp never came. Instead, a slight tremor rumbled through the ground beneath Grumpty's feet, and opening his eyes he looked around puzzled. The vibrations began to increase in intensity and the Wolf King paused, sniffing the air inquisitively.

Lowering his paw he turned and scanned the treeline behind the Haggard Wolf. Shouts and cries could be heard in the distance, accompanying the low rumble. The trees and bushes trembled and shook violently. The Wolf King's eyes widened and for the first time in the cruel animal's life fear overwhelmed him.

A moment later there was a tremendous crash and several enormous Forest Trolls charged into the clearing, their loud roars shaking the trees. As they thundered their way towards the centre of the clearing the Wolf King darted swiftly to the left, narrowly avoiding being crushed by one of the Forest Troll's gargantuan feet. The Haggard Wolf was not so lucky and suffered a harsh blow from one of the troll's clubs, sending him flying through the air and yelping in pain.

The sleeping wolves woke suddenly and being caught off guard they scattered frantically to and fro, disorientated and disorganized. Many of the young grey wolves escorting the Wolf King lay in crumpled heaps on the ground, whimpering feebly. Grumpty, Ogle and his mother watched in amazement as the huge trolls stormed after the panicked wolves.

Seeing his company disbanded and fearing defeat close at hand, the Wolf King advanced upon one of the smaller trolls. He let out a menacing snarl and leapt through the air, his teeth sinking into the tough bark of the troll's leg. The troll roared in both surprise and pain and hopped around the clearing, trying to shake the Wolf King free.

Noticing their leader's fearless behaviour, a few wolves joined in, latching themselves onto the troll's other leg and back. Great tufts of moss were ripped from the troll's back, and eventually after much protest the towering creature was dragged to the ground. Enamoured by the Wolf King's success the remaining wolves broke into small packs of threes and fours and began attacking the invading trolls.

The three petrified elves made a dash for the edge of the clearing, ducking and weaving their way between troll's legs and over fallen wolves. Although a fairly large percentage of the wolves had been defeated due to the trolls' element of surprise, their tactic of forming small groups of attackers had paid off and more and more trolls were overpowered by the aggressive wolves.

All of a sudden, the Haggard Wolf appeared in front of Grumpty, blocking his path. The jet-black creature was limping, his back leg injured from the previous attack. Instinctively, Grumpty stood in front of Ogle and his mother despite the tight knot of fear in his stomach.

The Haggard Wolf growled and sprang towards the elves. Grumpty turned his back to the approaching wolf, protecting Ogle and his mother from the oncoming attack. He let out a high-pitched squeal as the Haggard Wolf's jaw clamped around his leg, yanked him off his feet and started to drag him along the ground.

He clawed and scrambled in the dirt, desperately trying to cling on for dear life. Ogle darted forwards and grabbed hold of Grumpty's arms, pulling him in the other direction. Grumpty shrieked in pain as the Haggard Wolf dug his paws into the ground and wrenched him free from Ogle's grip.

Suddenly, without warning, a large vine net landed over Grumpty and the Haggard Wolf. Ogle shouted in triumph as he spotted two pixies high above, grinning devilishly. Glancing round he noticed more of the winged magical creatures zipping to and fro. Some of them carried other large nets between them, crafted from vines and roots. Others fired small darts from tiny bamboo tubes.

The wolves they managed to hit, slowed, tripped and remained still. Shocked by his current predicament, the Haggard Wolf released his hold on Grumpty, allowing the small elf to crawl out of one of the gaps in the net. Ogle raced over to his injured friend and dragged him away from the furious Haggard Wolf who was thrashing about wildly in the tangled net.

Aided by the arrival of the mischievous pixies the Forest Trolls fought back against the wolves with renewed strength. The Wolf

King snarled at the flying pixies and jumped up and down, snapping at them irritably. Distracted, the Wolf King didn't register an approaching troll and howled in pain and astonishment as he was booted hard in the flank by the large creature's foot.

He soared through the air and collided with a nearby tree. The wolves looked around, completely dumbfounded at the sight of their wounded master lying at the bottom of the tree. Seeing them off guard,the trolls and pixies rushed forwards at the wolves in a combined effort. Leaderless and outnumbered the remaining wolves retreated carrying away their fallen leader with their tails between their legs.

Grumpty lay on the hard ground, staring up at the moonlit sky above him dotted with pixies. He could hear muffled voices nearby, but they were too distorted to understand. His leg felt hot and throbbed dully, and try as he might he couldn't find the energy to sit up and have a look. The world around him became hazy and his eyelids grew heavy. High above several shadowy shapes soared over the tall treetops. Grumpty's lip curved into a smile and then everything turned black.

CHAPTER 7:
THE FEAST

Grumpty's eyes slowly flickered open. Thin strands of sunlight filtered through a canopy of leaves high above him. He lay still, drinking in the warm oranges, browns and greens that swamped his vision. The powerful glare of the sun backlit the forest ceiling, allowing Grumpty to observe the wispy skeletal lines running through the leaves.

A slight breeze ruffled the canopy and one of the auburn leaves came loose, slowly spiralling and drifting its way down towards the half-awake Grumpty. It landed gently on his cheek, tickling his skin. Usually, such a thing would have irritated him, but in his current drowsy state he couldn't have cared less.

A small dark shadow flitted past the leaf canopy and Grumpty blinked, trying to dispel his bleariness. A moment later the dark shadow reappeared and hovered behind the screen of leaves. Grumpty narrowed his eyes and could discern a long, thin shape extending from the shadow's head.

He could also make out a blurred movement from either side of the shadow and realized with the slightest of smiles, that it was a pair of beating wings. Contented, Grumpty closed his eyes and allowed sleep to take hold.

~~~

When Grumpty awoke, sometime later, he found himself in more familiar surroundings. The bedroom of his treetop house to be precise. He let out a loud yawn and rubbed his tired eyes.

Something creaked to the right of him breaking the serene silence, and glancing round he was surprised to see the sleeping form of Ogle nearby. He was curled up in Grumpty's wicker chair, dozing quietly. The chair rocked back and forth gently on the spot. Grumpty stared at Ogle curiously, recalling his first encounter with the young elf.

Grumpty had snuck into Father Mugleaf's orchard, a knap-sack slung over one shoulder in search of top-quality acorns. To his surprise he had discovered Ogle and a few other accomplices gathered around one of the large trees, picking and collecting as many acorns as they could find.

Ogle had spotted Grumpty hiding unsuccessfully in a small bush and had dragged him out by his feet. He had then proceeded to hang Grumpty upside down from one of the tree branches. Father Mugleaf had discovered him a while later, a pile of acorns gathered underneath him.

Deeply angered, Mugleaf had marched the red faced Grumpty home to his parents, who, gravely embarrassed and disappointed, had grounded him for two weeks solid.

Grumpty returned his attention to the sleeping elf before him and considered how much had changed since that day. Ogle had shown a side to him that Grumpty had never seen. Courage, love, commitment, dependency, fear. All traits that Grumpty would have never associated with Ogle.

For the first time in years Grumpty felt that he could begin to forgive the elf and his history of bullying. Not enough to become friends. Not yet by any means. There was still a lot of damage to be repaired.

A sudden thirst consumed Grumpty. His throat was dry and coarse, and he was reminded of the Rock Troll in HoneyGlade. Perhaps that was why he was so hostile. A throat made out of rock had to make swallowing difficult. His eyes darted around the room, looking for a source of water to quench his thirst.

In the corner there sat an oak dressing table. Balanced on its edge there stood a large tankard. Hoping above all other hopes that the tankard contained some form of hydration, Grumpty went to lift his head from the pillow and winced as a sharp stab of pain coursed through his right leg. He looked down at it and frowned. A large piece of bark had been strapped around the front, bound up with long strands of vine.

Grumpty felt a hand on his shoulder and looking round came face to face with a concerned looking Ogle. In his hand he held the large tankard. To Grumpty's relief it was filled with water, and laying back he allowed Ogle to carefully tip it between his lips. Grumpty eagerly gulped down the water and when the tankard was nearly drained, he let out a huge burp.

Feeling a little more rehydrated and relieved he let Ogle assist him into a seated position. His leg throbbed and ached and no matter what position he sat in it still hurt a lot. With no memory of how he came by his injury, Grumpty asked Ogle to illuminate him on the situation. As Ogle began to recount the events of the battle at the clearing, the images started to seep slowly back into Grumpty's mind.

~~~

The door flap was pulled back and Grumpty hobbled out onto his veranda in the early evening sun. Two large T shaped sticks had been placed under his armpits to serve as makeshift crutches. There was a tremendous cheer as Grumpty emerged from the leaf covered tree house. The bright sunlight blinded him for a second and all he could see were dark shadows.

When his eyes slowly readjusted, he was astounded to see an enormous crowd gathered below him. All manner of creatures had converged in the area. Elves, Forest Trolls, Tree Pixies, even a few owls were perched in the surrounding trees. Slightly over-whelmed, Grumpty raised his hand and waved at the massive congregation.

~~~

Grumpty sat at the end of an incredibly long and ornate oak table in the centre of the glade. Elves, pixies and trolls sat and hovered on the surrounding tree stumps, chatting merrily to one another. A mouth watering feast had been prepared in celebration for the heroes' return, and the table was heavily laden with sumptuous piles of food.

Grumpty watched the celebrating creatures all around him, his leg resting on a dandelion pillow atop the table. Never had these three races interacted with one another in such a sharing and communal way. The unification of these creatures under the same cause had not only brought about the defeat and exile of the wolf tribe, but also helped form strong alliances and bonds between the races.

Grumpty spotted Ogle and his mother halfway down the table and at that moment felt an overwhelming sense of loss for his own mother. He forced down the emotions that were threatening to consume him and waved at them merrily, putting on a brave smile. They returned the gesture, rosy cheeked and happy. The pain in Grumpty's leg put a slight dampener on his own celebrating but his mood was suddenly improved a little when he spotted Father Mugleaf sitting at the far end of the table, watching the festivities around him with a disapproving eye.

Nut was sat next to him trying to push a cup of acorn wine into his hand. Arms crossed, Mugleaf shook his head adamantly. Grumpty chuckled and popped a gooseberry into his mouth. Barkle was stood under one of the nearby trees, trying his best to woo a rather unimpressed female elf. Azral was nowhere to be seen and Grumpty scratched his head, puzzled by his friend's absence.

A hoot from above made him look up and Grumpty spotted Mother Owl perched on one of the tree branches. The younger owls were dotted about in the accompanying trees. Owls are very reserved creatures. Although friendly by nature and willing to help in a crisis, they generally keep themselves to themselves. Grumpty was slightly disappointed that they weren't more involved in the celebrations, but respected their decision and was grateful that they had chosen to make an appearance at all.

Glancing at Mother Owl he was surprised to see her beak moving, and squinting up at the branch he noticed that an elf was sat beside her. It was Azral. Since the two had worked together to provide air support for the battle in the clearing they had become close friends. Grumpty put it down to their shared knowledge and appreciation of Finhorn Forest.

Still, it was surprising to see Mother Owl being so talkative with an elf. Grumpty felt a tug on his tunic and looked down to see one of the elflings peering up at him with eager eyes, like saucers. In his hand he held a piece of bark and a sharpened twig. Grumpty took the bark and using the twig etched his name into the surface. He handed it back to the elfling, who eagerly admired it and ran off excitedly.

~~~

The next day the village of elves woke late and having slept in well past lunchtime, they collectively shared in a hangover to end all hangovers. A few Forest Trolls that were too tired to return home had collapsed onto the forest floor and still remained there snoring loudly as the elves slowly emerged from their dwellings and begun the arduous task of clearing up.

Grumpty was nowhere to be seen. No one was particularly concerned, presuming that Grumpty had slept in late to rest his leg. By early evening however, there was still no sign of Grumpty, and the elves gathered around the mossy stone to discuss the situation. Only a handful knew where Grumpty was and they had been sworn to secrecy. Before the celebrations the previous night, Grumpty had pulled the five elves, whom he had journeyed with, to one side and told them of his plan to leave with the owls at dawn.

Life had changed a lot for Grumpty in the village and since his return he finally felt appreciated and respected by his fellow elves. However, the village had never felt like a home to him. He belonged with the owls. His first glide above the treetops had been the most exhilarating and breath-taking experience of his life ever since that day he had gotten the taste for it. It was not the only reason.

His adventure with the other elves through foreign regions and lands, had opened his eyes to new and alien ways of life. He was desperately eager to explore more and by following the owls, he would be able to do just that.

~~~

Mother Owl soared across Lughorn Lake, accompanied by her young owlets. It was a foggy morning and the mist curled and twisted around and beneath her wings as she flew through the air. Grumpty lay atop her feathered back on his front, his small arms gripping tightly on to her neck. He closed his eyes and smiled as the fresh spray from the lake flecked his face. Opening his mouth, he yelled at the top of his lungs and felt the cool morning breeze ruffle his sandy hair.

~~~

The company of defeated wolves stood silently in front of their fallen master. The great Wolf King lay still on the grassy ground, his eyes glassy and vacant. The Haggard Wolf sat back on his hind legs, arched his neck back and omitted a large wounded howl. The surrounding wolves joined in and soon the forest rang loud with the sounds of howling.

The Haggard Wolf lowered his head and slowly the howls began to peter out. He turned to face the company of wolves, a deep, fierce fire aflame in his eyes. He let out a low menacing growl, vowing to seek revenge upon the cursed elves.

PART 2

CHAPTER 1: THE FUNERAL

A ceremony was held in tribute to the Wolf King's passing the same night that the great battle against Grumpty and the elves had taken place. The large animal's body would have fallen prey to carrion birds and other scavengers, if arrangements hadn't been made that evening. Four young wolves with immensely broad backs and thick front legs had set about digging a hole in which to bury their master.

It was hard work, not helped by the fact that the weather was extremely humid, and the poor beasts were tired from the fighting. Despite the fatigue the four diggers pushed on, ignoring the sweat running down their brows and stinging their eyes.

The Haggard Wolf watched them silently. Three other wolves stood guard over the body of the Wolf King; their large eyes fixed on the treeline for any signs of hungry intruders. Wolves were feared among many races of the forest, and it was unlikely that any creature would have the courage and audacity to try and steal the Wolf King's carcass. However, their defeat at the hands of a group of peaceful elves might have changed things. Creatures such as the trolls and pixies could look to capitalize on that loss, and launch an attack on the wolves while they were weakened.

One of the digger wolves was beginning to tire, his large paws dragging out less and less loose earth with each scoop. The hind legs of the animal were shaking with the effort, but he tried to carry on regardless. To give up now would result in him suffering ultimate shame and he would be punished harshly for his lack of loyalty and commitment to the cause.

It was true that the Wolf King was dead and although no wolf would openly admit it, it brought a sense of relief. Cruel was an understatement when applied to the Wolf King. Unfortunately, the Wolf King's demise left the responsibility of leadership to fall temporarily on the flea-bitten shoulders of the Haggard Wolf.

The emphasis being on temporary, as there would inevitably be a challenge for the title of king from another wolf at some point. For the time being though, the Haggard Wolf would assume control and having been the Wolf King's right paw for quite some time, had a similar approach to leadership.

The struggling digger wolf was fumbling the earth clumsily and one of his back legs wobbled alarmingly for a moment, before somehow managing to remain upright. Not for very long though. The Haggard Wolf snarled loudly, bearing his long yellow teeth and suddenly sprang forwards.

He charged head-first into the weak wolf, the force of the attack catching the digger wolf off guard and sending him rolling across the ground. The other diggers paused in their fervent clawing of the soil to see what was happening. The Haggard Wolf barked loudly, his command echoing through the clearing and hurriedly the observing diggers returned to their task, attacking the earth with more urgency this time.

The Haggard Wolf threw a disgusted look at the digger he had just bowled over, before setting to work on the hole himself. The other wolves in attendance watched the digger limping away from the pit, their hungry eyes drawn to the weak creature in their company.

The Haggard Wolf would never admit it in front of his company but for the first time in his life he was scared. Not of the elves. It was true he had underestimated them as had his master, but fear hadn't come into it. What he did fear was what was to come next.

It was fast approaching nightfall, their leader was dead, they were all weak and tired and their numbers had dwindled considerably. The Haggard Wolf was a proud animal and a fierce fighter, but even he had the sense to know when the odds were against them. One didn't get to be the right-hand advisor to the king without having the intelligence and foresight to plan ahead.

So, the beast pushed on, digging deeper and deeper into the ever-widening hole, encouraging his fellow wolves to follow his example.

When the hole was finally deemed deep and wide enough, the four wolves stood aside to allow the next part of the burial preparation to take place. Their fur was damp and glistening with sweat and even the Haggard Wolf joined in with the panting, as the observing beasts sat down and watched the proceedings. The Haggard Wolf had so much dirt and earth smeared on his face and paws, that he looked like he had been buried himself.

He glanced apprehensively at the ever-darkening sky. It was on the cusp of night, when it is neither blue nor black, but has a purplish hue to it, giving a distorted, dream like quality to everything. The next stage required three more specific wolves, commonly referred to as Breakers.

They were chosen among other wolves, as they possessed larger skulls and broader foreheads. Usually used for ramming attacks during siege warfare, their skills would be utilized for a different reason.

They were given the task of moving the Wolf King from his position on the grass to the hole they had excavated. It wasn't too far, as the Haggard Wolf had thought it only sensible to dig the pit near to where the deceased animal lay. They took up their positions, one wolf in the middle and the other two at the sides.

Then they lowered their heads, pressed them up against the Wolf King's immobile body and began to push with all their strength. Slowly, the dead weight body of the Wolf King rolled over and the Haggard Wolf acknowledged it with a bark of approval.

Even with three strong wolves it was hard work. The Wolf King had been an unusually large animal with incredible strength. During the canine's youth, he had grown at an exceptional rate, shooting ahead of his fellow cubs in both height and weight. Eventually after much effort, the three breaker wolves gave one final collective butt of their heads against the Wolf King and the large beast tipped over and fell heavily into the open hole.

The central breaker glanced at the Haggard Wolf, who inclined his head to indicate his work was done. There was a deep silence, as the Haggard Wolf padded forward and sat on his hind legs in front of the open grave. It was usually customary fashion to hold a few minutes silence for the fallen warrior before howls of honour were enacted.

They all waited in silence, some bowing their heads respectfully, others closing their eyes and a handful simply eyeing the open grave morosely. The Haggard Wolf observed his fallen master throughout the silence and when the allotted time had passed, called over another four wolves. He scooped up a paw full of dirt and threw it onto the Wolf King's body.

The message was clear. There would be no howls tonight. Every animal in the company knew it was too risky and could attract unwelcome attention. As the four wolves began scooping and piling the disturbed earth back into the hole, the Haggard Wolf walked to the edge of the clearing and raised his head.

Far off in the distance, a set of formidable grey mountains lined the horizon, their snow-covered peaks obscured by the looming clouds. A sleek, thin wolf with silvery grey fur appeared by his side and observed him for a moment before scanning the mountains herself.

Bile formed in her throat as she realized what the Haggard Wolf intended to do next. She wanted to object but knew that it would make no difference. The Haggard Wolf had already made his decision.

~~~

Grumpty woke in a cold sweat with sharp shooting pains in his leg. For a moment he just lay there immobile, trying to slow his panic strickened breathing and elevated heart rate. Then with a great effort, he sat up. The surrounding darkness of the tree hole

that served as his sleeping quarters, was only partially illumin-
ated by a slither of moonlight shining through the opening.

Some of the bedding of grass and ferns had become temporarily glued to his back, due to his excessive sweating. A large leaf
was draped over the leg which had been causing Grumpty such
discomfort and hesitantly he pulled it back. A large sigh of relief
escaped his lips, as he observed his throbbing leg in the half light.
It was just normal residual pain from the battle.

With a huff and a groan, Grumpty climbed to his feet and took
a moment to brush off all the loose bits of grass and fern attached
to his tunic. His muscles felt heavy and stiff and very much protested as he hobbled over to the entrance and squinted out into the
night.

A long branch extended out from the hole and perched halfway along it was Mother Owl, her great yellow eyes scanning the
forest floor below them. Grumpty sighed and began to make his
way over to her. Feeling the shift in weight on the branch, Mother
Owl swivelled her large head around and her chest bulged alarmingly, seeing the small elf wobbling slightly as he approached.

Noting her expression Grumpty gave her the thumbs up, indicating he didn't need help. It wasn't graceful but Grumpty eventually managed to reach Mother Owl without plummeting to the
forest floor. He sat down next to the majestic tawny creature, his
stumpy little legs hanging over the edge of the branch and pushed
the hair out of his eyes.

Mother Owl regarded her adopted son quietly for a moment.
She knew that some of the other owls stared at him with curiosity
as he looked so different, but they never dared to speak up about it.
Grumpty was a part of the family now and that was that. The little
elf grimaced and massaged his sore leg. Mother Owl said nothing.

Though her son would never openly admit it, he was still
suffering from the encounter with the Wolf King. The pain in
Grumpty's leg was one aspect, but Mother Owl believed it was the
psychological trauma that was preventing her son from sleeping
soundly. Grumpty tried to recall the dream he had been having
that had caused him to toss and turn so much throughout the

night.

It was a little hazy and fragmented, but he remembered running through a darkened forest at one stage. Something had been following close behind but Grumpty had dared not turn around for fear of what it was he would see. It wasn't clear what had happened but next thing he knew he had been on the ground, sprawled out on his back.

A large dark shape had stood over him blocking out the light, and although Grumpty hadn't been able to identify the shadow the deep guttural growl that had emanated from it was all too familiar.

Grumpty shivered, as the Wolf King's face suddenly loomed into his thoughts. Mother Owl, who was still observing him silently, presumed it was due to him being so clammy and sweat ridden. She moved closer to the small elf and took him under her wing. Grumpty didn't protest, glad for the comforting presence of his surrogate mother.

A distant flapping noise made Mother Owl look up in time to see a small grey owl flying hurriedly towards their tree. The owl landed lithely further down the branch and hopped over to her. Grumpty was still concealed under her wing and couldn't hear what the two owls were saying to one another.

The branch beneath them bounced up and down a bit, indicating that the grey owl had departed once more. Mother Owl lifted her great wing away and Grumpty felt the cool night breeze buffet against him once more. He looked up at her and felt a sudden uneasiness in his gut. There was something deeply troubling about Mother Owl's expression and Grumpty wasn't entirely sure he wanted to know what it was.

~~~

The company of wolves had pushed on hard throughout the night, only pausing momentarily to allow themselves a brief stop to recover their strength. It was dark now and all the wolves were deeply fatigued, except the Haggard Wolf and the silvery grey She-

Wolf. They were leading the pack and had apparently managed to break through the wall of exhaustion, such was their determination to reach their goal.

The digger wolf that had been openly humiliated had fallen behind and had only been able to keep up with the assistance of some of the other wolves. The grey formiddable mountains grew closer and the Haggard Wolf became more excited with each pad of his paw. The silvery She-Wolf on the other hand eyed the nearby summits with an expression of deep unease.

The clouds that had lingered overhead, threatening rain, had moved on, leaving in their place a carpet of sparkly stars. Coupled with the strong glare of the almost full moon, the Haggard Wolf felt extremely exposed despite being under the cover of the tall forest trees.

Owls hooted in the canopy above and occasionally the wolves noticed dark shapes shuffling around in the undergrowth. The Haggard Wolf pressed on, trying to ignore the fact that possible hidden threats lurked in the trees around them.

Much to the company's relief, excluding the She-Wolf, the pack emerged from the trees onto a long stretch of open grass. At the other end of the sloping hillside stood the rocky mountains. Set into the foot of the first mountain was a large, dark and imposing cave mouth. The She-Wolf resisted the urge to turn tail and flee and stayed close to the Haggard Wolf's side, as he led the procession of canines over to the entrance.

It was only when they had stopped in front of the opening that the Haggard Wolf realized there was a large iron door blocking the cave entrance. He turned around to face the company of wolves. Many were still standing, although panting heavily and overcome with exhaustion. Others had given up on ceremony and had collapsed on the ground, resting their furry heads on the slightly damp grass to cool their body heat.

The Haggard Wolf caught sight of one of the breaker wolves and barked at him. Hearing he had been summoned, the breaker wolf padded over and waited patiently by his leader to receive his orders. The Haggard Wolf leant in and whispered the commands into the fellow animal's ear. The breaker nodded dutifully and trotted over to the large heavyset iron door.

Lowering his great head, he shifted into a secure stance, then with pure brute force he headbutted the solid door with his powerful forehead. The Haggard Wolf eyed the treeline behind them anxiously, feeling certain he had glimpsed something moving in the shadows.

After a few moments, the Haggard Wolf repeated his demand and the breaker wolf butted the large door again, this time drawing blood from his forehead. One of his fellow breaker brethren huffed loudly in disapproval, but didn't pursue the matter further when the Haggard Wolf threw him a challenging look.

The breaker wolf prepared for another attempt but at that moment a loud clang reverberated throughout the large door. Fearful of what lay on the other side, the breaker returned to his place at the rear of the company. His fellow breaker brothers licked at his bloodied wound compassionately. There were several louder clangs and then the towering iron door began to open slowly outwards.

Despite being a little apprehensive, the Haggard Wolf moved closer to make out what lay on the other side. At first, he presumed the door was operated by some sort of mechanism, but as it swung open he saw that four muscular dwarves were pushing against it.

The Haggard Wolf glanced sideways at the She-Wolf and saw she was eyeing the darkened tunnel beyond the door with much trepidation. The thought didn't fill him with much comfort either, but at this moment in time, they had no alternative.

The four dwarves had pushed the door open wide enough to allow entry and stood eyeing the wolves curiously. The Haggard Wolf started forwards, trying to appear casual, his head thrust out proudly in front of him and moved into the tunnel with a confident stride.

After a moment's hesitation, the She-Wolf followed and then the rest of the company of wolves fell in behind them. The tunnel was very dark, and even with their keen eyesight the wolves struggled to make anything out. As the last wolf of the procession passed over the threshold, the four dwarves began to pull the door shut behind them.

The She-Wolf growled deeply, having the uncomfortable feeling that they were walking straight into a trap. The Haggard Wolf silenced her with a snap of his jaws. From further down the tunnel several lights could be seen bobbing towards them. It was just as well because the large iron door was nearly shut now, and it was becoming even harder to see.

The sound of shuffling feet approaching from the darkness made their ears prick up, and a moment later several more dwarves came into view. They were all carrying purpose made torches, the flickering light casting a golden glow against the tunnel walls.

A loud boom reverberated around the cave as the door was heaved shut, and the accompanying gust buffeted the torches. The Haggard Wolf was about to move forwards, when another noise stopped him in his tracks. It was a sound that filled wolves with a deep dread and their collective fur coats bristled with alarm.

One of the dwarves had unsheathed her sword, the all too familiar sound of the blade being drawn from its scabbard. There was a moment of deathly silence then the sound started again, but this time in unison. The Haggard Wolf's blood ran cold with fear. He had led them into a trap.

CHAPTER 2:
DWARVES

After being ambushed in the tunnel entrance, the wolves had been shepherded at sword point to a holding area, which contained four prison cells. All of the company, apart from the Haggard Wolf and the She-Wolf had been forced into the cells and secured under lock and key. Four of the dwarves were left behind to guard the prisoners, while the remaining handful escorted the Haggard Wolf and the She-Wolf further into the heart of the cave.

After passing through a network of low roofed catacomb like tunnels, they emerged out into a huge cavern. Great towering pillars of stone rose up to the cavern roof and worker dwarves moved around the large chamber, seeing to their various jobs.

Some of them were chipping away at the walls and floors with large pickaxes, others were wheelbarrowing around ore and other materials, and a handful could be seen stationed here and there on various stages of scaffolding that had been erected.

In the middle of the room, at the top of a tall flight of stairs cut from the natural stone of the cave itself sat an ornate iron throne with symbols and icons engraved into its surface. Seated upon it was a dwarf adorned in impressive black armour. She watched the two wolves ascend the stairs slowly, a concierge to her right whispering into her ear quickly.

The Haggard Wolf and the She-Wolf were struggling with the oppressive heat that frequented the cavern. Its source was a huge furnace set right at the back of the chamber. Despite the seated dwarf being dressed in full body armour, she didn't seem affected by the heat. The She-Wolf desperately wanted to pant to cool herself down but refrained. She didn't want to show any sign of supposed weakness in front of the dwarves.

As they reached the top of the stairs and moved towards the dwarf occupying the throne, the Haggard Wolf observed what was in front of him. Two dwarves stood either side of the seated dwarf, eyes forward and standing to attention. The one on the right, who had been whispering earlier, was an elderly female dwarf with silvery grey hair and a wrinkled, leathery face.

The one on the left was a young female dwarf with large eyes and smooth pale skin. The dwarf on the throne was younger than the silvery haired elder yet older than the pale faced youngster. She looked like she had seen a few battles, evidenced by a nasty scar on her left cheek. But there was an alertness in her eyes that indicated she hadn't been ruling the dwarf kingdom overly long.

It presented a funny image, as it depicted three stages of a female dwarf's life: adolescence, middle age and seniority. The dwarf who was sat upon the throne cradled a black helmet in her lap, which matched her body armour. Perched on top of her head was a silver crown, with a striking emerald gem in its centre. The Haggard Wolf knew of the Dwarf Queen, mainly by reputation and was not entirely surprised by her appearance.

Although no major wars had been fought during her reign, it hadn't been an entirely peaceful period under her rule and a number of smaller battles had taken place. The most notable being an attempted coup by some of her own dwarves, but she had quashed that rebellion before it had developed into something more serious.

'You are either very brave to walk into my domain or very foolish. I am more inclined to guess the latter.'

She had a deep, resonant voice and the She-Wolf now understood why the dwarves had developed a reputation as accomplished singers. The Haggard Wolf said nothing and glanced around at the escort of dwarves that were stood nearby, watching them guardedly.

The Dwarf Queen tented her fingers and contemplated the two

wolves. Underneath her silver crown she had long, thick auburn hair that came down to her shoulders. Her eyebrows were bushy and close together, which gave the impression that she was permanently frowning.

It was hard to tell how much bulkier the armour made the Dwarf Queen look, but the She-Wolf presumed she was pretty stocky underneath it anyway. Her eyes, which were small and beady, were dark brown verging on black, and served for an extremely penetrating stare.

'I come with a proposal,' said the Haggard Wolf, and even though he wasn't being aggressive it came out as a snarl.

Once again, the elder dwarf leant in to say something to the Dwarf Queen but was dismissed with a wave of her hand. The royal advisors spoke wise words, but they could only make suggestions. It was the Dwarf Queen's decision whether to listen to them or not. The Haggard Wolf glanced at the elder dwarf who looked a little put out, before returning his gaze to the Dwarf Queen.

'Continue,' she said, gesturing with her hand.

The Haggard Wolf looked at his She-Wolf companion, who appeared extremely unhappy about the whole situation. He understood her reservations, but their options were limited, and it was too late to turn back now.

'An alliance between wolves and dwarves,' the Haggard Wolf said plainly.

The Dwarf Queen erupted into laughter and the young advisor on her left let out a small giggle. The elder dwarf remained stony faced, no doubt thinking it was unprofessional to laugh in the presence of royalty. But the Dwarf Queen wasn't a traditional ruler, hence the reason there had been a coup.

When she had been crowned, the Dwarf Queen had brought into effect some rather radical ideas and a small collection of dwarves had not been happy about it. Catching sight of the Haggard Wolf's expression she stopped laughing.

'Surely you're not serious?'

The Haggard Wolf inclined his head, indicating that he was. One of the escort dwarves moved closer to the She-Wolf but quickly stepped back when the animal emitted a low threatening growl.

'Our races once fought side by side against the elves or have you forgotten our ancestors so easily?' the Haggard Wolf remarked snidely.

The Dwarf Queen's face suddenly flushed hot with anger and she gripped the arm rests of her throne tightly.

'Watch your tongue wolf or I will dispense of it with my sword.'

The Haggard Wolf didn't break eye contact but neither did he argue. It was imperative that he gain the dwarves' support, and although he took no pleasure in biting his tongue it proved necessary for the greater good. The Dwarf Queen untensed her fingers but her expression remained severe.

'I do recall the great war and I remember the terrible price my people paid against the elves. Why would I seek to repeat such accursed history?'

The She-Wolf's heart sank. The dwarves would never agree to an alliance. It was common knowledge that the cave dwelling race were an insular and self-contained people. After the carnage of the war and a bitter defeat, they had retreated to the mountains to lick their wounds.

Over time they had rebuilt and regrown, and gained a fearsome reputation once more. But they were a cautious race and seldom ventured out of their mines, preferring to remain in the dark confines and turning most of their attention to developing their industry.

Knowing that the Dwarf Queen would never agree to such terms, the She-Wolf began looking around. They had come with the whole purpose of recruitment but if the dwarves refused, and they would, there would no longer be any need for the wolves. They would either be imprisoned like the others or worse yet, killed and eaten. The She-Wolf's fur coat bristled at the thought.

'Because we need to eliminate the elven threat once and for all,' the Haggard Wolf explained, taking a small step forwards. 'We need to eliminate the elven threat once and for all.'

One of the escort guards went to intervene but the Dwarf Queen flapped at her to stand down.

'Are you not forgetting the peace agreement our three races signed?' the elder dwarf said, speaking up for the first time.

Usually a dwarf advisor was not permitted to speak so brazenly but the Dwarf Queen allowed it. It was a valid point and she was interested to see what the Haggard Wolf's response would be.

'I do, but I believe that particular peace agreement was broken when our former Wolf King was slain by an elf.'

A ripple of shocked gasps passed through the assembled dwarves, and the Haggard Wolf couldn't help but give a sly smile at the impact his words had caused.

'What are you talking about?' the Dwarf Queen said hotly.

'You really should venture outside more often. While you have been mining and crafting, my company and I have been embroiled in a battle,' the Haggard Wolf replied.

Even the She-Wolf couldn't help but smile at her companion's clever skills of persuasion.

'Why would an elf risk the peace we have sustained? To what end I ask you?' the Dwarf Queen demanded.

'Truthfully I know not the reason. We were ambushed by them at night. Perhaps they saw an opportunity to destroy us once and for all,' the Haggard Wolf said, purposefully neglecting to mention how the wolves had kidnapped an elf prior to this.

'But they didn't defeat you entirely?' the Dwarf Queen remarked.

'No, Fortunately I and a handful of wolves managed to escape from the chaos. We ran all night to reach you,' the Haggard Wolf further detailed, again altering the truth quite liberally.

'You mean to say that you could have led them right to our door,' the elder dwarf shrieked suddenly.

The Dwarf Queen was about to reprimand her for the outburst when it dawned on her what the advisor had just said.

'Were you followed here tonight?' she said, clenching the armrests tightly.

Now he had gone and done it, the She-Wolf thought to herself.

His mistake had been to continue to lie. The trick to any con was to find something that was true and tweak it ever so slightly. The Haggard Wolf had tweaked too much and it had backfired on him, quite spectacularly.

'I believe we lost them. I didn't see any sign of them just before we arrived,' the Haggard Wolf stammered, feeling the heat from the furnace intensify.

'We both know elves are good climbers and soft footed. Just because you didn't see them doesn't mean they were not there,' the Dwarf Queen said in conclusion.

The Haggard Wolf and the She-Wolf exchanged worried looks. The young advisor whispered something into the Dwarf Queen's ear, who nodded in response.

'I have heard enough for now. I need time to think and discuss this matter further with my council. You will return to your cells for the time being,' the Dwarf Queen commanded loudly.

The Haggard Wolf went to say something, but the She-Wolf brought her paw down upon his, and when he looked round at her she shook her head fervently. If the dwarves decided to form an alliance it would only occur when decided by the cave race themselves. They were stubborn by nature, and if the Haggard Wolf pushed too much, they might just refuse on a knee jerk reaction.

As the two wolves were led back down the stairs and through the winding, narrow catacomb like tunnels their train of thoughts were on very different tracks. The Haggard Wolf was trying to come up with a way to further convince the Dwarf Queen, if she declined their offer. The She-Wolf on the other hand, ever the realist, was trying to devise an escape plan in case things turned sour.

~~~

Father Mugleaf was watering the plants in the church garden when he heard a hoot in a nearby tree and glanced up upon hearing the noise. It hadn't been that long since Grumpty had left with the owls but Mugleaf already missed the small elf dearly. The vicar had always been a sort of father figure to Grumpty, as the pygmy elf's relationship with his real father had been complicated to say the least. He recalled the time Grumpty had visited him after school one day and the small elf had confided in him that he was being bullied.

Grumpty had changed so much since that day and had grown into a brave, strong and compassionate elf. Mugleaf's more pious side was happy for Grumpty, as he was certain that by leaving with the owls, he would experience the wonders that the world had to offer. At the same time, he worried for the small elf. While it was true that they had defeated the Wolf King and caused a devastating blow to the wolven forces, Mugleaf couldn't help but feel a lot of it had been luck. If it hadn't been for the Tree Pixies and Forest Trolls, victory would have most certainly eluded them.

Mugleaf trusted Mother Owl to do her best to keep Grumpty safe but the creature had a whole parliament of other owls to watch over. Mugleaf feared that Grumpty, emboldened by their victory over the wolves, would seek out more adventure too readily and possibly put himself in danger.

Approaching footsteps disturbed Mugleaf's train of thought and he glanced in the direction of the graveyard entrance. Ogle was wandering up the path, head bowed. Mugleaf waved at him but Ogle didn't notice, his attention still focused on the ground as he followed the path up, round and past the side of the church.

It was odd to see the young elf visiting the graveyard. Ogle wasn't exactly the type for quiet contemplation, but then again, ever since the party of elves had returned, he had been out of sorts. In truth they all had been. The morning after the celebratory feast, Mugleaf had stopped by Barkle the Inventor's house. He had been surprised to find Barkle sitting at his kitchen window, staring out into his back garden aimlessly.

Sat in front of him lay a half-built contraption. It wasn't unusual to see half assembled inventions laid out on Barkle's table, but what was peculiar was that this one lay untouched. The only time Barkle tore himself away from his work was to test out said equipment or scavenge for additional parts. The adventure had quite possibly been the longest time Barkle had spent away from his work. As such Mugleaf had presumed that Barkle would have been desperate to jump back into it.

Barkle had been pleased to see Mugleaf and had invited him in for tea. It had been nice to catch up at first but Mugleaf sensed something had been troubling Barkle. After a little bit of coaxing and gentle prodding, Mugleaf had learnt that Barkle was suffering from inventor's block. He had further gone on to elaborate that it had never happened to him before.

Mugleaf nodded thoughtfully and confided in Barkle that he also felt out of kilter and had been struggling to come up with a good sermon for his Sunday congregations. While both elves were glad to be back where they belonged, the grand adventure they had undergone had changed things.

The glade should have still felt like home, as it was the same old village it had always been. Mugleaf had come to the conclusion that perhaps they were the ones who had changed. The two elves that sat in Barkle's kitchen weren't the same two naive elves who had previously embarked on that adventure, and the realization of it had been slightly difficult to digest. Barkle had felt better after talking about it, but when Mugleaf himself had left the inventor's house he had felt a crisis of faith for the first time in his adult elf life.

Ogle had disappeared behind the church and Mugleaf wondered if he should go talk to him. But the young elf had looked like he wanted to be left alone. Elves came to the church to be alone with their own thoughts and Mugleaf didn't want to impeach on Ogle's quiet reflection. Satisfied that the plants had been sufficiently watered, Mugleaf set down the watering can and wiped his sweaty forehead.

It was a hot day and it didn't help matters that Mugleaf was dressed in his ceremonial robes. All the heat radiating from Father Mugleaf's body was suddenly replaced by an icy chill. A loud noise had broken the peaceful serenity of the hot summer day. It was the village's alarm horn.

After Ogle's mother had been kidnapped the elves had held a village meeting ,and decided it would be prudent to implement some sort of village alarm system. Then if any threat or danger occured, the village could be notified and the elves could try best to prepare themselves.

Mugleaf was already through the church gate, running down the path leading towards the village centre, when Ogle came quickly around the corner, a scared expression on his face. The watering can lay on its side in the flowerbed, its contents sloshing messily out on to the soil. A cloud moved over the brilliant blue sky, blocking out the amber sun and casting the graveyard in a moody grey shadow. Ogle shivered, as a chill breeze ruffled his clothes and hair.

CHAPTER 3:
THE DEAL

The She-Wolf paced anxiously back and forth behind the bars of the cell, occasionally glancing at the dwarf guards posted nearby. One of them caught sight of her and displayed a nasty smirk. She snarled in response, bearing her long and pointed teeth.

'Why is it taking so long?' she said, pausing her pacing and glancing to the back of the cell.

The Haggard Wolf was sat with his back to her, licking the wound on his leg. Although it wasn't a serious injury, the wound hadn't had a decent chance to heal following the battle, what with them running hard throughout the night. The Haggard Wolf must have been in pain, but he was concealing it well. The She-Wolf hadn't noticed any signs of discomfort on his face or a physical limp. But she suspected he was going to great lengths to make that appear to be the case.

'We must be patient,' the Haggard Wolf said, stopping his licking and studying the back wall of the cell in contemplation.

'I don't like all this waiting. It makes me unhappy,' the She-Wolf said and resumed pacing.

The Haggard Wolf couldn't help but chuckle.

'You are never happy.'

The She-Wolf thought about arguing but eventually shrugged the matter off. She was incredibly stubborn, but also recognised that the Haggard Wolf was even more stubborn, and it would be fruitless to bother arguing the point. Besides she knew she was a sceptical, suspicious and guarded wolf and it was the reason for her still being alive and well. Some of the wolves in the next cell over were barking loudly at each other, but soon fell into silence, when one of the dwarf guards banged loudly on the bars.

The She-Wolf studied the four dwarves left on guard duty. They all had short cutlasses and a few of them also had small cudgels on their belts. One of the dwarves with an almost permanently impassive face also had a ring of keys attached to her belt. The She-Wolf had been trying to figure out a way to acquire them, but without much success. The key holder was clearly the head dwarf and sensibly chose to remain further back from the cells than the rest of the guards.

She turned her attention to the cell around her instead, looking for possible weak points, but the cell looked strong and well maintained. This had been one of the main reasons the She-Wolf hadn't wanted to enter the dwarven domain in the first place. Dwarves were strong fighters and cunning warriors but they excelled in tunneling, mining, building and crafting best of all.

The cell around the two wolves would have been built solidly and to the highest standards. It was common knowledge that the dwarven cave fortress was practically impenetrable and now they were stuck inside of it.

'We should never have come here,' she said bitterly.

The Haggard Wolf sighed and closed his eyes. He was tired. The physical toll of the battle with the elves afflicted his body. The pain in his leg was slowly draining what little energy he did have, and it was a lot of effort to try and conceal his discomfort.

If he started limping or showing any signs of suffering, the other wolves would see it as an opportunity to challenge him for leadership. The Haggard Wolf was one of the strongest fighters in the company, if not the strongest, but his injured leg put him at a disadvantage. Better to maintain the facade and avoid that scenario altogether.

'Will you stop pacing,' he snapped. 'It is getting on my nerves.'

The She-Wolf glared at him.

'It's what we do and besides, I don't want to let my guard down.

Who knows what these dwarves are planning?'

She glanced at the dwarf guard who had smirked at her previously. The guard rested a hand lightly on the hilt of her sword, indicating that she clearly needed only the smallest of reasons to use it. The breaker wolves in the next cell over were wandering around their enclosed space, occasionally studying the bars and back wall.

No doubt trying to figure out strategic points of attack, like the She-Wolf had been doing. The breaker wolf who had cut his head against the main cave door sat in one corner, looking disinterested. He knew that even with the combined strength of all four breakers they wouldn't be able to smash through the bars. Even if they could somehow manage to achieve it, they would find themselves up against the dwarves. Perhaps all of them together could take them on, but not just one cell of wolves. The She-Wolf had considered going straight for the head dwarf if the opportunity arose.

She held the keys and if the She-Wolf could get to her, they had more of a chance. Her belly gave a low rumble. She couldn't remember the last time she had eaten but it must have been before the battle. The Haggard Wolf hadn't allowed the company to stop long enough to eat properly, such was his urgent desire to reach the safety of the mountains.

Earlier on, one of the dwarves had decided to sit in front of one of the cells and eat a leg of mutton. It had been excruciating for the wolves to watch, and when the dwarf had finished, she had thrown the bone into the cell. The wolves inside had fought over it ferociously, much to the dwarf's amusement.

The She-Wolf wondered if it was the dwarves' plan to starve out the wolves and let them eradicate themselves through hunger and cannibalism. She didn't want to give that idea too much thought, as she knew that when it came to survival of the fittest, she would resort to eat or be eaten as would her fellow wolves. As she turned to look at the Haggard Wolf, he was slowly getting to his feet and his leg faltered briefly for a moment before straightening out.

It had only happened for a split second and none of the other wolves had noticed, but the She-Wolf had. If the Haggard Wolf continued to make decisions she did not agree with, then she would have to seriously consider replacing him as leader. It was a risky move, but one she was more than willing to make if it meant securing the safety and longevity of the company.

Laughter filled the small antechamber. Two of the dwarf guards were sat at a table on the far side. Cards and metal chips were scattered over the wooden topped surface and the two dwarves were sat opposite each other, clutching hold of their own set of cards guardedly.

Several tankards took up the remaining space of the table and one of the dwarves was rosy faced and merry. The other guard sat on her own a little way away from the table, sharpening her cutlass. The key-holder was the only one paying the prisoners any attention and stood with her back to the wall, arms folded and expression impassive.

The sound of voices approaching from the tunnel made the keeper of the keys look up suddenly, and she kicked one of the seated dwarves in the leg. The dwarf grumbled in protest but when she noticed an orange light emanating from the nearby tunnel mouth, quickly stood up and motioned for the dwarf opposite her to do the same.

A moment later, three dwarves came around the corner, two carrying torches in their hands. The She-Wolf recognised one of the dwarves as the young advisor from the throne room. As they entered the ante chamber, she glanced round, as one of the guards accidentally banged his knee against the table. One of the tankards fell off the edge, hit the stone floor and rolled away, rattling loudly.

The key-holder shot the guard a murderous look, but the young advisor seemed unbothered. She casually motioned towards the nearest cell, which held the She-Wolf and the Haggard Wolf. The key-holder moved forward to unlock the cell door, one of the other guards behind her with her blade drawn, in case the wolves tried to escape. As the door swung open, the She-Wolf growled menacingly but shrank back when one of the torch-bearers moved inside the cell.

'You,' the young advisor said to the Haggard Wolf. 'The Queen requests your presence in the throne room.'

The Haggard Wolf inclined his head in agreement and moved through the open door, keeping a cautious eye on the nearby torch. Wolves hated fire with a fierce passion and for good reason. It was humans who had first figured out their fear for fire and used it to drive them back from attacking their settlements.

Glancing at the torch bearer to make sure she wasn't going to do anything unexpected; the She-Wolf went to follow the Haggard Wolf. The torch bearer barred her way, waving the burning stick dangerously close to the She-Wolf's face. Nevertheless, she barked at the dwarf guard angrily. The Haggard Wolf glanced at the advisor questioningly.

'The Dwarf Queen requests only your presence in the throne room. The invitation has not been extended to your bitch,' she said with venom in her voice.

All of a sudden, the She-Wolf butted the torch out of the guard's hand and wrestled her to the ground. Next moment she was on her, snapping and biting at the dwarf's uncovered face. The pinned guard tried to fight the animal off, but the She-Wolf was too strong.

'Let her go.'

The She-Wolf froze, her jaws clamped around the felled dwarf's head. The key-holder had her blade pressed up against the She Wolf's throat. The advisor was watching the proceedings with an expression of amusement, but the Haggard Wolf looked greatly displeased. Regrettably, the She-Wolf released her hold on the torch bearer and retreated.

The torch bearer scrambled backwards, flailing her arms wildly. She banged into the cell bars and sat slumped there, staring wild eyed at the She-Wolf. The key-holder kept her sword pointed at the She-Wolf, even though she had moved to the back of the cell.

The animal grinned devilishly, as the other torch bearer helped her traumatised comrade to her feet. The Haggard Wolf locked eyes with the She-Wolf and shook his head ever so slightly.

She got the message. This was not the time for fighting.

The assaulted dwarf crept gingerly over to retrieve her torch. As she scooped it up the She-Wolf snarled, and the dwarf with teeth marks and saliva covering her face hurriedly scuttled away.

The dwarves finished escorting the Haggard Wolf out of the cell and locked it behind them. The wolves in the adjacent cells, barked and howled in support of the She-Wolf's rebellious deed. The two dwarf guards who had previously been playing cards, moved forwards and banged their swords and cudgels against the cell bars.

It took a while to silence the enamoured beasts, but eventually they complied and fell quiet. The advisor exchanged low words with the key-holder for a moment, before signalling for the torch bearers and the Haggard Wolf to proceed into the tunnel.

The Haggard Wolf stopped at the tunnel entrance and glanced back at the She-Wolf. She was sat at the back of the cell and all he could see were her large green eyes, glinting in the shadows. Then one of the escorting guards shoved him in the hind with her cudgel and the Haggard Wolf reluctantly moved forwards.

As they moved through the tunnel, the Haggard Wolf felt his heart beat begin to quicken. The flames both in front and behind were making him uncomfortable. But it was more the fate that awaited the Haggard Wolf which caused him to be anxious.

~~~

The Dwarf Queen was pacing up and down in front of her throne when the escort detail reached the platform. All around them were industrial sounds, such as the hiss of the forge and the clinking of pick axes against rock. The first thing that the Haggard Wolf noticed was that the elderly advisor was absent. He tried to ascertain if that was a good or bad thing, but having not heard either of the advisor's words to the Queen it was too hard to tell.

'Have you come to a decision your highness?' the Haggard Wolf asked, hoping that his addressing of her as royalty would sweeten the deal.

The Dwarf Queen stopped pacing and eyed the Haggard Wolf

with a stern expression. For a moment he feared the worst and glanced around, trying to spot an escape route, but the dwarf guards blocked the path behind. It would be no good leaping off the edge of the platform. The fall was too steep and if he did somehow survive, he would certainly break his legs.

'My senior advisor tells me that it is a foolish idea to help join you in your fight against the elves,' the Dwarf Queen said, placing her hands on her hips.

'I'm guessing from her absence that you aren't entirely convinced by her argument,' the Haggard Wolf said shrewdly.

The Dwarf Queen gave a crafty smile.

'You are very perceptive. I can see why you are in charge of the company.'

The Haggard Wolf shrugged, not wanting to appear full of himself. The young advisor moved cautiously past the Haggard Wolf and resumed her place beside the throne. Unlike the Queen and her guards, she wore a simple black tunic with a silver axe image emblazoned on the front.

'My heart tells me not to pursue this course of action, but my head says differently,' the Dwarf Queen explained, glancing at her advisor who gave a respectful nod.

'And which do you choose to listen to, if I may be so bold?' the Haggard Wolf asked.

He wanted a simple answer, a plain yes or no. Then at least he would know what the score was. It was the waiting around to be told that was the truly excruciating part.

'I guess my biggest concern is the fact that the elves beat you. It is true, that we dwarves used to be skilled warriors, but that was a long time ago. My people are crafters, builders and engineers and seeking out a war with the elves could risk all that we have cultivated over the last hundred years,' the Dwarf Queen proclaimed.

The Haggard Wolf went to reply but the Dwarf Queen hadn't finished.

'You can't deny that they must have been a powerful force to best you and your company.'

The Haggard Wolf smiled slyly.

'Actually, I can.'

The Dwarf Queen looked both puzzled and intrigued so the Haggard Wolf pressed on.

'The elves weren't alone. They somehow recruited the Tree Pixies and Forest Trolls to aid them in battle. If not for them, we would have crushed the elves easily.'

'But if the elves have formed an alliance with those races, how do you propose we beat them?' the young advisor said, forgetting her place.

'Because it was but a temporary alliance,' the Haggard Wolf explained, before the Dwarf Queen could chastise her advisor. 'Once we were pushed back, the elves returned to their homeland. The last thing they will suspect is a counterattack after their victory. Furthermore, I know where they are based. It is a small village, home to families and civilians. If we strike now, we have the element of surprise.

The Dwarf Queen mulled this over in her head for a moment, before turning to her advisor to confer. The Haggard Wolf glanced over his shoulder at the two guards. They were watching him like hawks.

'I agree to your terms, but on one condition,' the Dwarf Queen announced loudly.

'Name it,' the Haggard Wolf responded quickly, unable to hide his eagerness.

'We will help you defeat the elves, in exchange for us being able to assume control over their village,' the Dwarf Queen put forth.

The Haggard Wolf was unsure as to why the Dwarf Queen would require or desire such land, but he didn't have time to dwell on such matters.

'Agreed,' he said, satisfied.

The Dwarf Queen snapped her fingers at the two guards.

'Release the prisoners, feed them and tend to their wounds. Your company have the night to rest. In the morning we set out for the elven settlement.'

The Haggard Wolf gave a wicked smile. He had vowed revenge on Grumpty and his kin and now it was time to deliver.

~~~

Nut and Barkle were sitting in front of the village pond, their feet submerged in the cool water and chatting casually away to one another when the village horn broke the air, signalling nearby danger. They both stared at each other, horror stricken for a couple of seconds, before they scrambled to their feet and started to run as fast as they could to the mossy stone. It had been the agreed rendezvous point for situations like this.

When they got there, a gathering of elves were already assembled. They were mostly young elves, but a couple of the older locals had turned up to fight for the cause. Azral was stood in front of the stone next to a large wooden crate, that was filled with a collection of makeshift weapons. Included were sharpened sticks, slingshots, bow and arrows and wooden clubs.

The assembled elves had formed a line and were stepping up one at a time to receive their weapons. Nut and Barkle joined the back of the queue and tried to catch the attention of Azral. But the elf was too busy hastily dishing out the weapons to notice his two friends.

Youngster elves and their parents were running to the safety of the treehouses at the back of the village. It was the safest place for the vulnerable and elderly, as it was high off the ground and away from the centre of the village.

'I've got to go,' Barkle said out of the blue and with no explanation whatsoever turned on his heels and ran off.

Nut shouted after his friend but Barkle paid him no attention. Instead he pressed on, making a beeline for his house. Although they had prepared a little, panic was rife in the air and Barkle had to weave and manoeuvre his way around blundering and hysterical elves running hither and thither.

Eventually, he managed to make it to his house and burst through the front door, his chest heaving up and down from the exertion. Shouts and hurried footsteps floated in through the open window, as Barkle moved into his living room and began rummaging through his cupboards and draws frantically.

After searching high and low for two minutes, throwing miscellaneous items and half-finished contraptions out of the way as he went, Barkle found what he was looking for. He studied the invention in the chest before him and prayed to the elf gods that it worked. After all it was a prototype, as were most of Barkle's inventions.

~~~

Nut finally reached the front of the line and had a club thrust into his hand, before Azral caught sight of his face. He grabbed the elf in a strong embrace, happy to see his friend. The touching moment was shattered when a series of loud howls broke the air, accompanied by some sort of dull thumping.

Both elves turned to look at the edge of the clearing. Through the trees, a dark shape was steadily approaching. It was walking on all fours and Nut and Azral knew instantly what it was. What they hadn't expected to see was another shape, this one upright.

It was short and stocky. As the two figures emerged through the trees, a cold shudder gripped the two elves. The Haggard Wolf stood at the edge of the clearing and standing next to him was an armour-clad dwarf.

CHAPTER 4:
THE SIEGE

Azral and Nut stared dumbfounded at each other, before returning their attention to the Haggard Wolf and the mysterious dwarf stood at the entrance to the village. There were no signs of any other wolves or dwarves nearby, but Nut had a suspicion that they were out there somewhere, most likely concealed in the trees.

Other elves had begun to notice the presence of the two intruders and had paused in what they were doing to observe. Much whispering and pointing was going on as a result of this. The two warriors were standing just in front of the screen of trees, watching the village silently. Azral wondered at the reason behind it.

The wolves had not hesitated in attacking when the elves had visited Sticklewood Huts, or when they had woken them in the clearing. Dwarven tactics he was less familiar with and suspected that perhaps it was their presence that was keeping the wolves at bay. He noticed that the crowd of armed elves were all watching him and Nut expectantly.

Azral looked to his friend for support, but the elf just shrugged unhelpfully. Sighing, Azral mounted the mossy stone and cleared his throat. The whispers and mutters of the assembled elves suddenly ceased, and their attention become raptly fixed on Azral.

'My fellow elves, I know you are scared, and I don't blame you, but remember what Grumpty showed us. That if one elf stands up to these bullies....'

'But they have dwarves with them this time,' cried a young nervous looking elf at the back.

Azral glanced at Nut and the older elf got the message. He scrambled up onto the stone and joined his friend on the make-shift podium.

~~~

The Haggard Wolf and the Dwarf Queen watched them from where they stood in front of the trees.

'I say we just attack them,' the Haggard Wolf said, pawing the ground impatiently.

The Dwarf Queen sighed and studied the animal beside her. She thought wolves were supposed to be clever, but this one was so hot-headed that she was surprised he had managed to survive so long. Dwarves used to be of the same mentality. That was back in the day when male dwarves had still been in charge.

Through their bullheadedness and arrogance, they had almost wiped themselves out in their attempts to invade regions and steal various lands from other races. It was the Dwarf Queen's great grandmother that had first introduced the rule to reverse the roles of power. Female dwarves had been given charge of policies of war, trade and foreign matters. In turn, the males were assigned to duties such as working and child rearing.

There had been some initial resistance, but the male dwarves soon came around to the idea. They got to remain in the familiar surroundings of the mountains, spending their time crafting and building.

'As I have said before, I want to attempt to do this peacefully. If we can persuade them to give over the elf you desire and surrender their lands, we both get what we want,' the Dwarf Queen explained.

The Haggard Wolf motioned to the village with a paw.

'They don't look like they want to surrender.'

The Dwarf Queen observed the crowd of elves in the centre of the village, with their makeshift weapons, and frowned. She wasn't afraid of a fight and would resort to it if necessary, but if there was a more sensible and effective way of solving the problem it was certainly preferable.

~ ~ ~

Nut cleared his throat and gestured at Azral, before addressing the crowd of elves gathered around them.

'We only need hold them off until we can get help. I propose we send a scout out to call for aid. The Forest Trolls and Tree Pixies provided support last time, and if we can contact Grumpty and the owls we will have an even better chance.'

There were a few murmurs from the elves, some seemed a little more satisfied by Nut's proposal, others still appeared unconvinced.

'Will any of you volunteer to seek out our allies and bring them back to help in the fight?' Azral declared, trying to convince the naysayers in the group.

Everyone suddenly grew very quiet and many of the elves became overly interested in their feet. They were afraid to fight, but the thought of leaving the village and entering the forest alone frightened them insurmountably more.

'The fate of all our lives depends on it. Will no one rise to the challenge?' Nut pleaded, appealing to the faces of the assembled elves, many of whom were purposefully avoiding eye contact.

'I will go.'

Several gasps broke the silence of the group. The voice had come from the back of the crowd and Nut and Azral couldn't make out who had spoken. The crowd parted like the red sea under Moses' command, and a serious faced elf approached the mossy stone. Nut and Azral both smiled in relief.

'Thank you Ogle...' Azral began, but a shrill cry suddenly cut him off.

A flustered looking elf was running towards them, flapping her shawl at Ogle accusingly. Nut let out a groan, as he recognised that it was none other than Ogle's mother. That was not good.

'No, no, no,' she shouted loudly, reaching her son and slapping him on the arm sternly.

Ogle flinched and massaged his arm, thinking that the dangerous forest seemed less of a threat than his overly protective mother.

'You can't send him,' she said stubbornly to the two elves stood on the mossy stone.

'I will be perfectly fine. I am probably safer out there than in here amongst the fighting. Plus, I rescued you, didn't I?' Ogle pointed out to her.

She ignored him and continued to stare fiercely at Nut and Azral. They were two of the hardier elves of the village, but even they quavered under her burning glare.

'Send someone else,' she demanded hotly.

'There is no one else. He is the only volunteer,' Nut said, but his voice lacked the conviction of his words.

Ogle's mother cast a furious eye around at the gathered elves and they shrank back, gripped by fear.

'Why don't one of you two go?' she stated plainly, turning her attention back to Nut and Azral.

Azral opened his mouth a few times, but no words escaped his lips. Seeing his friend struggling like a gormless fish, Nut spoke up for the both of them.

'We would but Grumpty left us in charge of organisation and distribution.'

Ogle's mother scoffed loudly with indignation. Azral was painfully aware of the Haggard Wolf and the dwarf still watching them. They couldn't stand here talking all day. For all Azral knew their enemies could be scoping out the village, planning where best to attack.

Ogle seemed to sense that time wasn't on their side, so he took his mother by the arm and coaxed her away. At first, she resisted, but eventually conceded. The crowd of elves watched intrigued, as Ogle whispered quickly and quietly to his mother a little way away. They were both gesticulating wildly.

Eventually, after a minute of bickering between the two, Ogle's mother nodded her head reluctantly and embraced her son in a tight hug. She left soon after that, most likely going to see if she could help with the very young and the infirm. Ogle returned to the mossy stone, his ears burning red from a combined mixture of embarrassment and having lost his temper a little.

'I've got the go ahead.'

There was a combined sigh of relief amongst the elves, as it sunk in that they wouldn't have to come up with an alternative solution to the quandary of the scout situation. Nut and Azral motioned for the designated warrior elves to come in closer and began laying out a plan.

~~~

Fed up with waiting and suffering from the pain in his leg, the Haggard Wolf had sat down. If he had to do as the Dwarf Queen desired and be patient, then he certainly wasn't going to stand around getting uncomfortable. The Dwarf Queen on the other hand remained standing. In her full jet-black battle gear the Haggard Wolf wondered how on earth she didn't melt.

'We've got company,' she said, gesturing with one of her stocky arms.

The Haggard Wolf raised his large head and spotted two elves approaching them from the village. The crowd from earlier had dispersed and this made the animal wary. They were vastly outnumbered, and their weapons were primitive, but even so the elves could be cunning when they wanted to. He recalled the trap they had set for him in Sticklewood Huts and inadvertently gave a low growl.

'Keep it together,' the Dwarf Queen muttered under her breath.

The elves had nearly reached them now and the Haggard Wolf suddenly recognised the two of them from Grumpty's rescue party. Unable to growl, he dug his claws into the ground beneath him. As they came to a halt just in front of them, Azral eyed the Haggard Wolf cautiously. Nut on the other hand was studying the Dwarf Queen closely. The four of them stood in silence for a moment.

A sudden gust of cold wind whipped up the leaves between them and sent the tops of the trees behind them into a frenzied dance. Azral's eyes left the Haggard Wolf's and came to rest on the dark and shadowy wood behind him. He instantly regretted his decision as he noticed dark shapes moving to and fro. Some low and slinking, others bulky and oddly shaped.

'I never thought I would see the day when a dwarf would venture to our lands,' Nut said, still observing the Dwarf Queen intently.

'Nor I, but here we are,' said the Dwarf Queen.

'What do you want?' Azral asked.

He hadn't meant to sound so blunt, but the presence of the formidable foes had rattled him somewhat and his emotions were running high. The Dwarf Queen looked a little irked and the Haggard Wolf went to move forwards, but she rested a hand gently on his crest. He begrudgingly remained where he was. Nut watched the exchange curiously, trying to understand the relationship between the two races.

'We are looking for an elf, or rather my associate here is,' the Dwarf Queen stated, gesturing to the Haggard Wolf.

Azral and Nut exchanged worried expressions. They both knew without her mentioning the name as to whom she referred to.

'He isn't here,' Nut explained, his mouth feeling very dry all of a sudden.

Azral shivered, which was odd because the cold breeze had long since passed. He felt extremely naked with just a cudgel for protection and eyed the Dwarf Queen's armour enviously, wishing he was better prepared.

'Where is he?' the Haggard Wolf said, his eyes alight with rage.

'We know not where. He left to be with his other family,' Azral said.

This wasn't entirely true. Grumpty had told him and Nut where he was going in case something like this were to happen, but he was dammed if he was going to betray one of his closest friends. The Haggard Wolf whispered something in the Dwarf Queen's ear, and she inclined her head in agreement.

'Tell us where the elf in question is and there will be no need for bloodshed,' she proposed.

'You're telling me that if we tell you where Grumpty is, you will leave peacefully and not attack us?' Nut said doubtfully.

There was a snapping of twigs in the trees and a few of the shapes shifted in the shadows. The orange glow of the sun behind the elves was providing just enough light to see clearly, but soon it would dip beneath the horizon and darkness would fall upon the land. Elves had fairly good night vision. It was important when you lived in a forest, but wolves and dwarves were natural night dwellers. The former hunted predominantly when the sun was down, and the latter spent all their time underground.

'We won't leave,' the Dwarf Queen replied. 'Because we require your land.'

Nut laughed in astonishment and Azral felt winded, like he had been punched hard in the stomach.

'And where are we supposed to live?' Nut stammered, out-raged.

'Oh, you are quite welcome to stay, and no harm will befall you, but ownership and deeds will be signed over to me,' the Dwarf Queen said, folding her arms.

Azral became painfully aware of just how big and muscled they were. He was nearly twice the dwarf's height but looking at her arms, Azral feared that it might not matter if she could break him in half like a twig.

'I will never give over our land to the likes of a dwarf,' Nut spat.

Azral was shocked by his friend's outburst. He knew the elf was older and it was more ingrained in him to dislike dwarves, but even so. The Dwarf Queen's hand reached behind her back to where her axe was strapped to her armour plating.

The two elves tensed, not sure whether to fight or turn and run. The Dwarf Queen caught sight of the Haggard Wolf watching her. He was grinning broadly. She lowered her hand and took a long, deep breath, trying to quell the anger bubbling up inside of her.

'So be it elf. Out of courtesy I will only attack once I have blown the horn,' the Dwarf Queen said, motioning to the ornate piece of ivory hanging off her belt. 'In response, I expect you to show us the same respect and not attack until the horn has sounded.'

The two elves nodded and turned to leave.

'Unless you have changed your mind that is? Last chance elves,' the Dwarf Queen called after them.

'See you on the battlefield,' Nut said over his shoulder, as the two elves walked back to the village.

'So, we are attacking them now, right?' the Haggard Wolf said, when the elves were out of earshot.

The Dwarf Queen rolled her eyes and turned, heading for the trees and her waiting troops. She was starting to wonder if joining forces with the wolves had been an unwise decision. It was true that the two races had once worked together, but that had been when male dwarves were still in charge.

In the past the alliance had made sense, as the male dwarves and the wolves were clearly both hot headed fighters. But the Dwarf Queen was different, as were her warriors, and she sincerely hoped that the Haggard Wolf would honour his end of the deal.

~~~

When Nut and Azral returned to the village the chaos had subsided somewhat, and the elves who'd volunteered to fight had taken up strategic positions. Elves had given up fighting many years ago and were now a strictly peaceful community. But archery was still a common sport and practised regularly. It had been Azral's idea to post a handful of them up in the trees with their bows. The trees were the highest points in the village and from there they would just be able to reach the first attacking row of the assault.

The ground troops were stationed in groups at several positions, reflecting the points of a compass. The village was painfully open to the elements and had no fence or wall surrounding it. So, the only option was to cover as many potential areas of attack as possible. At each of these defensive points they had stacked various items of furniture and piles of wood to form makeshift barriers. It wouldn't hold the enemy for long, but it would hopefully slow them down a little bit.

The biggest issue was the trees and church at the rear of the village. That was where the young and elderly had been put. More troops had been posted at this southern point, as it was essential that the vulnerable were protected. Unfortunately, that meant taking troops from other points, leaving these positions weaker.

Father Mugleaf had wanted to join his friends up front at the northern point. He was truthfully very scared but was willing to fight for his friends and community. Their original adventure had changed him and although still a pacifist by nature, Mugleaf had learnt on his journey the importance of fighting for the right cause. Azral and Nut were having none of it though.

Keeping the vulnerable safe was the number one priority and seeing as Mugleaf resided in the church, it was only right that he remain there with them. Mugleaf had been hugely opposed to this but when Nut and Azral had informed him that he would need to be armed and ready to defend if the enemy reached the church, Mugleaf had accepted and said no more on the matter.

The village looked completely different when all the nonfighting elves had been relocated to the church and trees. The hustle and bustle of a normal elven day had gone, replaced by a deep gulf of silence as the various groups of elves stood huddled behind their barricades. Nut was already up front at the northern position with his group and Azral was hurrying to his own post in the trees, when the noise of the battle horn broke the air.

He pushed on to his own group of elves, despite his legs feeling like lead. The sound of the horn had sent his body into overdrive, as panic flooded his body. Nut was stood behind the northern barricade, straining his eyes at the stretch of open grass that extended out from the village towards the tree line.

No one had emerged from the trees yet, but there was a rumbling sound emanating from somewhere. A tremble coursed through the earth beneath the elves' feet and Nut gripped his cudgel a little tighter. Apart from the ground shaking slightly and the increasing rumbling noise, the only sound to be heard was the the heavy breathing of the warrior elves.

Then accompanying the rumble, Nut could just make out the sound of yelling growing steadily louder. It rose in time with the rumble, until all the elves could hear it now. A moment later there was a terrific crash, as out of the trees came a truly terrifying sight.

The Haggard Wolf emerged first, and Nut's eyes took a moment to adjust to the image in front of him. On his back rode the Dwarf Queen, wielding her large battle axe and yelling at the top of her lungs. Following behind them were more wolves, each one with a dwarven rider on their back. The riders and beasts thundered over the open stretch of ground towards them. A few of the elves standing alongside Nut trembled.

'Hold steady,' he shouted over the roar of the charging animals.

From his position in the high branches of a tree, Azral observed the attackers quickly closing the gap towards the village. His hand was raised, and he held it there, waiting for the optimum moment to issue the order. Down below Nut glanced anxiously over his shoulder at the trees, painfully aware of how close the mounted dwarves were getting.

An overly nervous archer loosed a shot and the arrow thudded into the ground. It was way too premature, as the wolves and dwarves hadn't even reached that spot.

'Not yet,' Azral barked irately.

Nut wiped his forehead that was slick with sweat and planted his feet widely apart, cudgel ready for the attack to come. The main brunt of the force was heading directly for the northern barricade, but Nut noticed that a few had broken off and were moving to the left and right. He glanced at the elves stood alongside him and nodded at the pale faces looking to him for guidance. They returned the gesture and although it didn't remove the threat, it did bring some comfort to the elves.

'Fire,' Azral screamed, dropping his arm and there was a cacophony of twangs, as the archers released their arrows.

The shots rang true and a few of the wolves crashed to the ground, sending their riders flying into the air. The other shots glanced off the thick armour of the dwarves. The remaining members of the company powered on, despite a handful of their kin falling to the arrow. Azral also noticed some of the attackers breaking off to the sides and shouted at a few of the elves to focus on them. But try as they might the archers could not penetrate the tough armour.

'Aim for the mounts,' Azral instructed and this time the archers were more successful.

It wasn't quick enough, however. The attackers were moving at speed and it took time for the archers to reload after each volley. The Dwarf Queen leading the charge was bearing down on Nut's barricade, but the elf held his ground defiantly. Seeing his friend in danger Azral levelled his own bow at the charging Haggard Wolf, took a deep breath and fired.

There was a howl of pain as Azral's arrow buried itself into the Haggard Wolf's injured rear leg. The animal faltered for a moment and the Dwarf Queen prepared herself to bail if necessary. But somehow the Haggard Wolf pushed on, despite the arrow sticking out of his leg. Azral watched horrified for a second, then reached for his quiver. It was too late.

The Haggard Wolf smashed into the barricade, sending furniture and wood flying into the air. The Dwarf Queen had launched herself into the air before impact and barrelled into Nut, knocking him to the ground and sending his cudgel spinning away.

The clamour of steel on steel rang throughout the air and Azral watched on horrified, as more wolves carrying dwarves attacked the east and west barricades in a pincer like movement. This was exactly what the elves had feared. That by pulling some of the troops from the other points to defend the south, they had made themselves too weak elsewhere.

'Keep firing and focus on defending the barricades,' Azral ordered and picking up his own cudgel began nimbly leaping down the tree, expertly dropping from one branch to the next until he eventually swung off the lowest bough and landed in a half crouch on the ground.

The village that had previously been so quiet was now ablaze with noise. Elves and dwarves screamed, wolves howled and there were low thuds, as the breaker wolves butted fiercely against the barricades. Azral reached the north side of the village in time to see the Dwarf Queen swing her large axe, missing Nut's head by mere inches as he ducked out the way.

The Haggard Wolf was dealing with the rest of Nut's elves, who had surrounded the animal and were attacking him with their clubs. An unlucky elf got too close to the Haggard Wolf and the large beast seized him in his jaws, shook him around like a rag doll and threw him to one side, where he lay still.

Nut brought his cudgel down on the Dwarf Queen's head and it had glanced off her helmet like it was nothing more than a small stone. Seeing him on the back foot, the Dwarf Queen jabbed Nut in the midriff with the handle of her axe and the elf crumpled to the ground clutching his stomach.

Azral was halfway across the village towards his friend, when a loud scream erupted from behind him. Skidding to a halt, he spun round in time to see two wolves breaking down the church door. A handful of elves lay immobile on the ground nearby. Azral glanced back at Nut. The Dwarf Queen was advancing on him, her large axe in her hand. Arrows pinged and glanced off her armour.

More screams could be heard from inside the church. Azral did not know which way to go. If he went to help his friend, then he would be abandoning the defenceless elves now trapped in the church.

Alternatively, if he chose the church he might never see his friend again. There was the sound of things being smashed and knocked over in the church and more screams, accompanied now by ferocious growls. Azral, feeling terrible, made his decision and started off towards the church.

~~~

Ogle had waited until the siege had begun to slip out of the south east part of the village. Unlike the northern side, there was no clearly marked path leading into the trees. The woods to the south were on a gradient and led steeply downhill, but Ogle knew the way. Before Grumpty had left the village, he had taken Ogle down this route.

It had taken some time to carefully navigate their way down the steep incline, but at the foot of the hill of trees, it had levelled out into a small clearing. In the middle had been a strange and unusual looking object. Grumpty had revealed that it was yet another one of Barkle's inventions.

It had resembled an enormous shell, which had been placed upon a wooden box. Fixed to the side of it had been a hand operated crank. By turning it an owl-like noise would be produced through the shell. The size and shape of the shell meant the sound could travel over a great distance. If Mother Owl heard it she would know the village was in trouble and come to help.

The horn had already been sounded once but the elves had no way of knowing if it had worked. So, Ogle was going to try again and if that didn't work, venture out into the woods to find them himself. He was now halfway down the slope, slipping and sliding a little in his haste to reach the bottom.

The landscape was so steep and awkward that the elf doubted any wolves or dwarves would think to approach from this side. He was concentrating so hard on his footing and navigating, that Ogle didn't notice the wolf and mounted dwarf watching him silently from the top of the hill.

CHAPTER 5: THE TAKEOVER

The Dwarf Queen sat on top of the mossy stone, crossed legged, and observed the shackled elves shuffling back and forth in front of her. The Haggard Wolf was strolling around casually, occasionally snapping at slow moving elves. The two had successfully taken over the village, but their joint reign hadn't been without issue.

The Dwarf Queen had agreed that making the elves prisoners was a good idea, but had disagreed heavily with the wolves' desire to beat and humiliate the forest dwelling creatures. After a terse conversation where both leaders had been prepared to come to blows if necessary, the Haggard Wolf had eventually conceded. He still wanted Grumpty and knew that if he lost the support of the dwarves, he would be at a big disadvantage.

So far, they had been picking out elves at random, taking them into one of the elven huts and questioning them about Grumpty's whereabouts. The Dwarf Queen had assigned one of her best fighters to be present, to ensure that the wolves behave themselves. So far, they hadn't made great progress. The elves, although not the physically strongest race, were a resilient bunch.

They were an incredibly loyal and devoted people and the Dwarf Queen respected that. One of the things her late mother had taught her was to respect and never underestimate the enemy. Trying to prise out the much-needed information they required, the wolves and dwarves had attempted intimidation, threats and deals but so far no one had broken.

~~~

Ogle's plan to reach the alarm and call Grumpty and the owls for backup hadn't panned out. He hadn't even managed to make it to the bottom of the hill. The wolf and dwarf had caught up to him and dragged him back to the village.

When interrogated as to where he was sneaking off to, he had lied and said he was running away from the fight. Better that than they find the alarm and possibly set a trap for Grumpty. They needed the help, but he wasn't willing to risk the safety of his friend and the owls to do it.

Nut had survived his encounter with the Dwarf Queen, but just by the skin of his teeth. Or rather by a strip of cloth. When he had been lying sprawled out on the ground under the imposing form of the axe wielding Dwarf Queen, he had closed his eyes. Panic had gripped him, but he had also come to terms with the fact that he was going to die.

The large axe had swung down and Nut had felt the whoosh of air that came with it, but no pain. At first he had presumed that it had killed him instantly, but opening his eyes the elf had realised he was still alive. The Dwarf Queen had sunk her axe into the very top of his hood, pinning him to the grassy ground and missing his head by a hair's breadth.

When Azral had entered the church the scene had been pure chaos. The terrifed elves had been pushed to the back of the building by the advancing wolves, and pinned down with nowhere to run and nothing to fight with. The screams and cries had been as a result of the snarling wolves, biting and snapping at the air in front of them.

Azral had fought his best, but two of the wolves had overpowered him and had been closing in for the kill. Barkle had come to his rescue wielding a bizarre looking device that looked like a crossbow, but with a strange multi-pronged head.

It fired nets and the inventor elf had managed to bag three wolves before the dwarves piled in and captured them. Barkle had berated himself for not doing more, but Azral had pointed out that he had stalled the wolves long enough for the dwarves to arrive.

When Barkle, Nut and Azral were reunited, they had marvelled at how they were all still alive and came to the realisation that the dwarves seemed more intent on capturing than killing. They had also let the elves bury the handful of their kin who had unfortunately died during the battle. They had all decided that this information might well prove useful later on.

~~~

Mother Owl and her company of owls soared across the treetops beating their wings as hard as they could to cover as much ground as possible. Grumpty sat astride his mother's large neck, clinging onto her feathers for dear life. He usually enjoyed flying, but on this occasion the speed and bumpiness of the journey was more terrifying than thrilling.

At the same time he dared not ask Mother Owl to slow down. There was a reason for their hasty progress. The small owl that arrived the night before to talk to Mother Owl had brought grave tidings. As a scout it was the small owl's job to fly on ahead, scan out the area and make sure it was free of threats and dangers. The small owl hadn't discovered any nearby danger but had heard the sound of a loud horn being blown. It had come from the direction of the village.

By the time she had reached the village things were already not looking good. From the safety of one of the surrounding trees, she had observed the comings and goings. The dwarves and wolves had seized control of the small settlement. The small owl had seen a handful of the elves wandering about the village square and wondered if she had got the wrong end of the stick. But then with her keen eyes she had noticed that the elves were shackled at the feet and hands.

Dwarves were posted at various points of entry around the village, and a handful of wolves were patrolling the treeline in shifts. It was extremely lucky that the small owl had gone on ahead and heard the noise of the alarm. For whatever reason it hadn't worked as powerfully as they had hoped. Grumpty just prayed no one had been badly hurt. The fact that they had taken prisoners was deeply worrying, but it hopefully meant that they wanted them alive for some reason or other.

The company of owls set up position a little way back from the treeline, while Mother Owl, Grumpty and the small scout owl perched on the furthermost trees. There was a moment's panic when a patrolling wolf passed right under the trees they were sitting in. They drew a collective breath as she paused and sniffed the air around her suspiciously.

The sky gods must have indeed been smiling on them that day as the wolf soon strolled off continuing her route. The small owl had been right about the situation but sitting here observing it for himself, Grumpty saw just how dire things had become.

The wolves were a formidable force by themselves, but coupled with the arrival of the dwarves it spelt serious trouble for Grumpty and the owls. He thought about trying to wrangle together the Forest Trolls and Tree Pixies. It had worked last time. But Grumpty had a nasty feeling that they would be less keen to help out, knowing dwarves were involved this time round.

'What do you know about dwarves?' he asked Mother Owl.

Mother Owl contemplated his question, tilting her head to one side as she did so.

'Only what I have heard,' she replied. 'They set up home in the mountains long before my time. My father told me they were fierce fighters at one stage.'

Grumpty looked worried.

'But that was long ago when male dwarves were still in charge,' Mother Owl added.

Her attempt to comfort him was appreciated but didn't really help. They might not be the same army of dwarves, but their armour and weapons certainly looked the part. Grumpty massaged his forehead. The stress and anxiety of the whole situation had given him an acute headache.

He was trying to think up a strategy, but his head felt like it was full of fungi. His first thought had been to try rescuing them from the air. If they came from the sky, the owls could try and scoop up as many of them as they could before the dwarves and wolves realized their plan.

However, there was one major problem with the plan. Even if they could rescue his fellow elves, where would they go. The village was their home. It wasn't like they were sneaking into enemy territory. This was elven land. Plus, there was still the handful of elves that were being kept inside the church. Grumpty wasn't cutthroat enough to take some of his kin and leave others behind to their fate.

'What are you thinking?' Mother Owl said, watching her son thoughtfully.

Grumpty sighed and turned to face her.

'I've got an idea, ' he replied. 'But you're not going to like it.'

~~~

The She-Wolf was patrolling the tree line as usual when she noticed something white floating towards her from the trees. Puzzled, she sat on her hind legs and observed the object drawing nearer. Her keen eyes revealed that it was a feather. A moment later a small elf appeared out of the trees. In his hand was a long stick with the white feather stuck on the top. The first thing the She-Wolf noticed was that the creature was unnaturally small compared to most elves.

Then it suddenly made sense to her. This was the pygmy elf the Haggard Wolf had been trying to find. For a moment she just sat there regarding the small form of Grumpty in disbelief, taken aback at how he had just strolled up out of the blue. Then she darted forwards, knocked the stick out of his hand and pushed him to the ground with a paw.

Grumpty rolled over a few times and thumped into the sprawling roots of a nearby tree. He lay there for a moment, groaning. High above in the trees Mother Owl observed this and went to intervene, but the small owl blocked her with a feathery wing. The Mother Owl looked at her scout furiously but didn't go to push past.

Grumpty slowly got to his feet, brushing himself down. His elbow stung like hell from where he had banged it against the tree, and his leg protested with shooting pains.

'I come unarmed,' he said, holding out his hands peacefully.

The She-Wolf sprang forwards and opened her mouth wide. Grumpty recoiled in fear at the slavering jaws of death. The she-wolf's teeth sunk into Grumpty's collar and next thing he knew the small elf had been lifted off his feet. The She-Wolf turned and started running back towards the village, carrying the helpless elf.

She had wanted nothing more than to rip the tiny upstart into pieces, but knew that the Haggard Wolf would never forgive her. It was his prize and his alone. Mother Owl and the scout owl watched Grumpty being carried away by the sleek wolf and exchanged worried glances.

As the She-Wolf entered the village, a couple of the dwarves noticed Grumpty hanging from her mouth and watched their progress, intrigued. A nearby wolf noticed it too and began howling loudly. Soon the village was full of the sound of howls as the wolves fell in behind her, enamoured by the important discovery.

Barkle, Azral and Nut were sat among three other elves, all shackled, and guarded by two dwarves and a wolf. Hearing the noise, Barkle had got to his feet to see what was going on. One of the dwarves had sternly instructed he sit down, but the elf remained standing.

His view was blocked for a moment by a group of dwarves, who had wandered over to see what was happening. One of them moved slightly out of the way and Barkle glimpsed Grumpty just as the She-Wolf dumped him in front of the mossy stone.

'Sit down,' the dwarf shouted and pushed Barkle roughly down onto the ground.

'What are you doing?' Nut whispered, as he and Azral crawled over to him.

'It's Grumpty,' Barkle said, his eyes wide.

Azral and Nut exchanged surprised reactions, that then morphed into expressions of deep fear.

Grumpty landed on all fours and felt the hard ground shudder through his palms and knees. It was a sunny day, but the small elf shivered as he felt shadows all around him. His eyes travelled slowly up the mossy stone, continuing up the Dwarf Queen's mammoth legs and broad chest, until they came to rest on her resolute face.

'So, you are the famous Grumpty I have heard so much about,' she said after a moment's pause.

Grumpty said nothing but looked around terrified at the crowd of gathered wolves and dwarves surrounding him on all sides. The wolves were snarling and growling loudly, but the dwarves were quiet. They just observed the little elf curiously, as if he were some sort of unusual piece of art.

The Dwarf Queen held up a hand, willing the wolves into silence. They obliged but didn't look particularly happy about it. She opened her mouth to speak but was interrupted as the Haggard Wolf barged past two dwarves and made a beeline for Grumpty.

Despite being petrified the small elf rose to meet him. He knew some of the elven prisoners would be watching him and he had to stand up for them. Like it or not he was a symbol of hope for the village community. If he bowed down and showed cowardice the wolves and dwarves would win. The Haggard Wolf stopped mere inches from Grumpty's face and gave a deep, menacing growl. The small elf fought back the urge to retch from the big wolf's hot, bad breath.

'Let us hear what the small elf has to....'

The Dwarf Queen never got to finish her sentence as the Haggard Wolf lashed out with a clawed paw. It struck Grumpty across the face and he fell to the ground, blood seeping from the fresh wounds left there.

A roar of laughter erupted from the gathered wolves as the Haggard Wolf moved in for a second strike. But he suddenly found his way barred by the Dwarf Queen as she dropped down from the mossy stone and thudded into the ground before him.

'Move out of my way dwarf,' the Haggard Wolf barked, fury alive in his eyes.

But the Dwarf Queen held her ground, her large feet planted firmly and her hands on her hips. The Haggard Wolf was a force to be reckoned with, but the Dwarf Queen looked equally as formidable.

'I wish to speak to the elf privately for a moment,' she said.

The Haggard Wolf's face morphed from one of fury to disbelief. He glimpsed Grumpty, who was still lying on the ground. He was rolling around, clutching his face in his hands and moaning in a low voice. While seeing the small elf in pain brought a certain level of satisfaction, it just wasn't enough.

'This wasn't part of the deal,' he snarled and tried to push past her.

The Dwarf Queen didn't budge but fixed him with a firm stare.

'The deal still stands. I am a woman of my word. I just want a moment alone to talk to the elf. When I am done, you may do whatever you want with the creature.'

The Haggard Wolf thought for a moment. He looked at the She-Wolf, who was watching the exchange keenly. She shrugged as if to say what harm could it do. The Haggard Wolf glanced around at the village. Elves sat in little groups guarded by dwarves and wolves.

They were trying their best to see what was going on, but the guards kept purposely blocking their view and pushing them back down. The She-Wolf was right. What was there to lose? If it meant that the Dwarf Queen would stop pestering him then it was worth it. The surrounding dwarves and wolves watched silently as the Haggard Wolf inclined his head and stepped aside.

'Follow me elf, I wish to speak with you,' the Dwarf Queen ordered and strolled off towards one of the huts.

Grumpty let his hands fall from his face and fought back a wave of dizziness as he caught sight of his palms that were slick with blood. His face stung badly, and he could feel the blood trickling down his nose.

As the crowd parted to let the Dwarf Queen and Grumpty past, the wolves and dwarves showed a combination of revulsion and amusement at the elf's face. He had no idea what he looked like, but presumed it was pretty hideous based on the spectator's reactions.

Grumpty tried to fight back tears but it was practically impossible. The three long gashes on his face stung so badly that his eyes watered heavily from the intensity. The blood dripping down his nose felt hot and sticky. He wiped at it with his moleskin sleeve and only ended up smearing more of it over his face.

'Grumpty,' a familiar voice shouted, and the small elf blinked away tears to see who had called him.

An elf was signalling to him a little way away from the middle of a group of seated prisoners. He squinted hard and recognised the familiar face of Azral waving wildly at him. Grumpty went to wave back but paused as a dwarf guard approached Azral, forced down his arm and pushed him roughly to the ground. Enraged, Grumpty caught up to the Dwarf Queen.

'Tell your guards to stop being so rough with the elves,' he demanded hotly.

The Dwarf Queen raised an eyebrow in mild surprise but didn't say anything and continued walking. She reached one of the huts and poked her head through the entrance to check it was empty.

'Why are you helping the wolves?' Grumpty asked the Dwarf Queen.

She answered by grabbing him roughly by the collar and throwing him inside the hut. He hit the ground, knocking over one of the wooden stump chairs and made an audible oomph noise in the process. So far it had been a day of being tossed around, thrown to the ground and mauled.

The Dwarf Queen joined him inside, located one of the still upright wooden stumps and sat down heavily. The stump creaked worryingly but held. Grumpty re-righted his seat and sat down. The Dwarf Queen watched him silently before reaching into a pocket and pulling out an ornate engraved pipe.

'Things have changed since you have been away little elf,' the Dwarf Queen said, as she stuffed tobacco into the pipe hole and started tapping it down.

'Clearly,' Grumpty said, touching one of the marks on his face tentatively and wincing as the pain intensified in the tender skin.

The Dwarf Queen regarded the elf's wounded face for a moment but not with disgust. Grumpty was surprised to see concern in her expression. Reaching into her other pocket she produced a handful of dock-leaves and threw them into the small elf's lap.

'Thank you,' Grumpty said with a mixture of caution and surprise, accepting the leaves.

He sat there staring at them blankly for a moment. The Dwarf Queen laughed, as she lit her pipe and sucked on the end of it a couple of times.

'It helps if you look inside,' she said, exhaling a big puff of smoke.

Feeling a little silly for not realising, Grumpty unfurled the leaves carefully. In the middle sat a small solid white ball. He touched it gingerly and was surprised to find it was both sticky and smooth at the same time.

'Rub that into your wounds. It will slow the bleeding and prevent them from becoming infected,' she instructed.

Grumpty nodded and began tentatively massaging the mysterious balm into his wounds. It stung something awful and his already watery eyes began to well up even more. Despite this he persevered and for a moment the two just sat there, Grumpty applying the balm and the Dwarf Queen puffing away on her pipe.

'Thank you,' Grumpty finally said, covering the balm back over with the leaves and offering it back to the Dwarf Queen.

'Keep it. You will need to apply it a lot more if you want those wounds to heal properly,' she said, exhaling another cloud of thick smoke.

It had become incredibly murky and dingy in the hut since the Dwarf Queen had started puffing away on her pipe.

'Why are you helping me?' Grumpty said, coughing slightly from the thick smoke trying to sneak into his nose and mouth.

The Dwarf Queen shrugged nonchalantly and cast an eye around the elven hut. It was the definition of rustic and simple. All that occupied the space was four tree trunk stools, some oak furniture and a few ornamental decorations on the wall, made from bones and leaves.

It was funny to see such a primitive and basic way of life. The Dwarf Queen was accustomed to lavish furnishings made of rich materials like metal and iron. They were also much bigger and grander in design. A dwarf's piece of furniture could take up three quarters of the elven hut's space.

'Just because you're my enemy, doesn't mean we can't be civil,' she said, observing the elf with a discerning eye.

'Your friend, the Haggard Wolf doesn't share those sentiments,' Grumpty said, gesturing at his battle wounds.

The Dwarf Queen looked slightly uncomfortable before quickly concealing her expression, but it was too late. Grumpty had already seen her face. It was rather telling he thought to himself.

'Yes, well each to their own I guess,' the Dwarf Queen reflected.

Grumpty wanted to take a deep breath but he was afraid that it might result in him descending into an uncontrollable coughing fit.

'What is the deal between you two anyway? You must have done something mighty serious to anger the wolves,' she proposed.

Grumpty laughed and immediately regretted it as the muscle movement caused his wounds to flare up again.

'The wolves blame me for the death of their master, the White Wolf.'

The Dwarf Queen raised her eyebrows in surprise.

'Yeah exactly, now you understand,' Grumpty said plainly.

The Dwarf Queen shook her head slowly. Grumpty unbuttoned his moleskin coat and loosened his collar. It was getting hot and the dense smoke was making the small elf feel a little woozy.

'I still don't get why elves would choose to pick a fight with wolves in the first place?' the Dwarf Queen pointed out, motioning with her pipe.

Grumpty frowned hard and again it sent a jolt of pain through his face. Why did he have to be so blooming expressive?

'We didn't,' he exclaimed.' The wolves started all this.'

The Dwarf Queen paused mid puff, her face deadly serious all of a sudden. She removed the pipe from her mouth and sat forwards. Grumpty recoiled at the dwarf's fierce expression.

'What are you talking about?'

'They started this whole thing off by abducting Ogle's mother,' Grumpty said, surprised that the Dwarf Queen wasn't already aware of this.

For a moment the Dwarf Queen said nothing but just sat frozen in her seat, regarding Grumpty with a completely dumbfounded look.

'Do you even know who you have partnered up with?' Grumpty asked the immobilised Dwarf Queen.

She turned her gaze towards him but didn't say anything. It was like the Dwarf Queen hadn't even registered his words and her eyes were vacant, looking right through him.

Grumpty was just wondering how long her paralysis would last when the Dwarf Queen suddenly stood up, knocking over her stool in the process. Grumpty went to open his mouth, but before he could say anything the Dwarf Queen had stormed out of the hut.

The Haggard Wolf and the She-Wolf were discussing matters to themselves when nearby shouting made them glance round. An enraged Dwarf Queen was storming towards them with powerful strides. A little way behind trotted Grumpty, who was finding it hard to keep up with the fast pace the angered dwarf was setting.

'Liar,' the Dwarf Queen roared, and such was her fury that a group of wolves in her path scattered hurriedly.

The She-Wolf snarled, preparing herself for a fight but the Haggard Wolf held up a paw to calm her.

'Not yet,' he whispered under his breath.

'You never told me that you abducted an elf in the first place,' the Dwarf Queen proclaimed, and a few gasps of surprise issued from the onlooking dwarves.

'It must have slipped my mind,' the Haggard Wolf said, trying to act casual.

'I wouldn't have agreed to this alliance if I had known foul play was afoot,' the Dwarf Queen stated and a few of her loyal troops voiced their agreement.

'Oh please, don't try and act like there is no bad blood on your hands,' the Haggard Wolf fired back and there was a smatter of agreement from the nearby wolves.

All eyes were on the two leaders as they exchanged spiteful words. The tension of the situation was palpable and some of the spectating dwarves and wolves eyed each other cagily. The hostility between the two commanders had been building for some time and it was about ready to explode.

Azral, Nut and Barkle sensed it too, and exchanging silent nods began to slowly crawl away from their spot. The assigned dwarf guards should have been keeping an eye on them but the heated confrontation had distracted them.

'My ancestors are guilty of terrible crimes, but we are different. It is true that there is no love lost between us and the elves, but I cannot persecute a race for an action they did not commit,' the Dwarf Queen declared.

Grumpty was stunned by her words and for the first time in his elven life, he felt respect for a dwarf. As a young elf, he had been raised to fear and not trust the creatures by his elders. But seeing the Dwarf Queen defend the elves despite her actions, made him seriously consider re-evaluating his ideals.

Azral, Nut and Barkle were making slow progress, choosing to slide forward on their stomachs so as to go unnoticed. Everyone was too busy watching the terse exchange to even register the escaping prisoners. Only Ogle spotted them wriggling across the grass towards the edge of the village. They motioned at him to follow but he just shook his head and remained seated with the other elf prisoners.

'What are they doing?' the scout owl said to Mother Owl, as they watched the situation from the trees.

'I don't know but it doesn't look good. Tell the others to be prepared just in case,' she responded, a pensive look in her eyes.

~~~

'We had a deal,' the Haggard Wolf snarled and the She-Wolf barked to reinforce the point.

The Dwarf Queen folded her arms resolutely.

'The deal is void. You left out a vital piece of information. My agreement was based on the fact that the elves had done you wrong.'

'What difference does it make?' the Haggard Wolf protested.

'It makes all the difference,' the Dwarf Queen thundered.

The Haggard Wolf thought for a moment and then spoke in an incredibly underhand sort of way.

'And what about the village? Without us it won't remain under your control for long. The elves have friends everywhere. In the trees, in the air. Trust me I found that out the hard way.'

This gave the Dwarf Queen moment to pause. The Haggard Wolf was right. If she broke the alliance with the wolves, then with it went the control of her new territory.

'Just give us Grumpty and we will ensure the village stays firmly under your control,' the She-Wolf propositioned.

Despite having spoken out of turn, the Haggard Wolf paid the interruption no heed. She had adequately articulated what he had wanted to say anyway. The Dwarf Queen eyed the two wolves shrewdly for a moment before turning to face Grumpty. She moved close towards him, and although intimidated the small elf held his ground. Leaning down, the Dwarf Queen spoke in barely a whisper.

'Free as many of the elves as you can and make for the trees.'

It took a moment for Grumpty to process what she had said, then he turned on his heels and started running.

'What are you doin....' the Haggard Wolf began but trailed off, as he saw the Dwarf Queen slowly unclip her axe from her back and turn to face him.

So, it was going to be like that he thought to himself and letting out a tremendous howl, bounded forwards to face his opponent.

CHAPTER 6: TOOTH AND NAIL

Grumpty had just kept running. When the Dwarf Queen had instructed he leave, the small elf had realised what was about to happen. However, it had taken a few minutes for the observing dwarves and wolves to process exactly what was going on.

The Dwarf Queen had swung her axe around in an arc towards the Haggard Wolf. The four-legged animal had just managed to avoid being decapitated, but some of his fur had been sliced off when he had ducked down out of the way.

He had retaliated by jumping forwards and clamping his teeth around the Dwarf Queen's arm. It was encased in armour, but the wild animal hung on defiantly as she tried to shake him off. The dwarves and wolves had watched stunned as the two leaders grappled with one another, before diving into battle between themselves.

For once Grumpty's short stature really came into play as he ducked, dodged and dived his way through the village. The dwarves and wolves didn't seem particularly interested in attacking the elves but rather each other.

Even so, it was hard work for Grumpty to navigate a course through the fighting. Once or twice he was knocked down as a wolf barged past him, or a dwarf staggered backwards into his path. The clearing rang loud with the sounds of shouts and growls, and deep booming thuds as enemies were felled or hurled into the sides of the huts. As Grumpty ran for safety, he waved madly at the prisoner elves to follow his example.

Most of them had seen fit to do so, but a few of them were rooted to the spot with fear. One particular elf, that Grumpty recognised as the village cook's son, was stood stock still as chaos reigned around him. Grumpty seized him by the arm and pulled him out of the way of a spinning dwarf trying to detach a wolf clinging to his back.

'Make for the trees,' he told the young elf, who despite being a foot taller than Grumpty quivered in his moleskin boots.

The elf nodded but didn't move and eventually Grumpty had to give him a shove in the right direction. That seemed to do the trick, as the elf woke from his panicked daze and set off as instructed.

'Grumpty,' a familiar voice called from somewhere to his left.

The small elf glanced that way and saw Barkle, Azral and Nut waving at him madly. Dwarves and wolves were fighting in front of them and Grumpty gritted his teeth, assessing the best way to get through to his friends. One of the dwarves drove a spear through a wolf's belly and lifted the creature high into the air.

Grumpty saw an opportunity and sprinting forwards like a march hare, he zipped beneath the impaled wolf that was still held aloft. Grumpty had timed it well. The body crashed into the ground soon after. It was too early to relax however, as a big dwarf landed heavily in front of him. Grumpty was moving at some speed and stopping suddenly would probably do more harm than good.

Thinking fast he jumped, landing lithely on the dwarf's helmet and launched himself into the air almost immediately. Barkle, Azral and Nut watched, slacked jawed, as Grumpty flew through the air. Elves were known for their acrobatics and climbing skills, but this was something else. It all suddenly looked very dire however, when a wolf appeared beneath him.

The animal opened his mouth, waiting expectantly for his approaching aerial meal. In the nick of time a dwarf appeared out of nowhere, seizing up the wolf in her big arms and driving the animal sideways and out of the way. Grumpty braced himself for the impact of the ground and landed in a half roll, cushioning a bit of the impact. Still it played havoc on his legs and arms. He rolled several times before coming to a stop at Azral's feet.

'Hello,' he groaned and allowed the three elves to help him to his feet, 'It's been a while.'

His legs and arms were shaking and Barkle and Nut held on to him for a while, until he felt steady enough to stand. They embraced quickly, happy to see each other despite the circumstances.

'Are you able to move because the trees are just there, and it isn't safe here?' Nut asked pensively.

'I can move,' Grumpty said and smiled bravely.

'Great let's....'Azral began but Grumpty held up a hand.

'But I'm not leaving.'

The three elves huddled around him exchanged perplexed expressions.

'We have to leave Grumpty. We aren't cut out for this. Look at how the dwarves and wolves fight,' Barkle explained, gesturing at the fighting taking place in front of them.

Barkle was right. The wolves fought with a hungry ferocity and played dirty, scratching, biting and kicking whenever possible. The dwarves fought more honourably and their brute strength was impressive to say the least. They were also very well trained with close combat weapons.

'I know it's suicide but there are elves who still need my help, and the Dwarf Queen did save my life. I can't just up and leave knowing that,' Grumpty stated, eyeing his three friends in turn.

'You owe that Dwarf Queen nothing,' Nut commented, 'Correcting her own mistake doesn't prove anything.

Suddenly, a dwarf's helmet bounced along the ground and glanced off of Barkle's right foot. He let out a shriek of surprise and started hopping around, gripping it in both hands.

'I've got to go help. Elves are getting hurt left, right and centre and the National Elf Service is pushed to the limit,' Grumpty said, motioning at Barkle, who was now sat on the ground inspecting his throbbing toes to make sure nothing was broken.

Grumpty glanced around and saw one of the dwarven swords. It was large and heavy, but he managed to drag it over to the other three elves. They were able to lift it between them and begin breaking the shackles that were still attached to their feet and hands. A dwarf was swinging a wolf around by its tail dangerously close by. Nut hurriedly moved out of the way as the wolf swung near him.

The dwarf let go and the wolf sailed through the air and disappeared into the trees. She turned to face the four elves and they all shrank back. After regarding them silently for a few seconds the dwarf moved away, most likely in search of another wolf for tossing.

'See you lat...' Grumpty began but trailed off when he caught sight of his three friends.

They were holding the chains from their shackles, like they were some sort of makeshift weapons. They didn't need to explain that they were staying behind to help Grumpty fight. It was obvious from the expressions on their faces. Azral handed Grumpty a section of the chain and nodded.

'Let's get our village back,' Grumpty said and the four elves moved forwards in their small unit.

~ ~ ~

Mother Owl flapped her large wings, beating the air like a steady drumbeat. The scout owl began to hoot loudly and soon the trees around them were full of the sounds of owls hooting and screeching. Mother Owl was the first to alight from the trees, followed by the scout owl, and then the rest of the airborne squadron fell in.

The air was soon full of the winged creatures as they soared towards the village. From up high Mother Owl and her company could see the overall situation of the fighting. It was pandemonium. Wolves and dwarves were locked in fierce combat while elves were fleeing desperately to the safety of the trees. Many of the huts had been demolished in the fighting, and dead wolves and dwarves littered the ground.

Mother Owl's instructions were to target the wolves first. The scout owl pointed out that neither were to be trusted but Mother

Owl had insisted. There were two reasons for this strategy. Firstly, the wolves were easier targets, as they wore no armour and carried no weapons.

Secondly, their reasons for fighting were more fuelled by revenge than their dwarven opponents. Mother Owl had seen the Dwarf Queen attack the Haggard Wolf. It was no clear indication that she had changed allegiance, but Mother Owl wanted to wait and see.

A small group of elves were running in the opposite direction to all of their other kin. Mother Owl gestured with one of her wings. The squadron separated. The scout owl leading half of them in one direction and Mother Owl in the other.

~~~

Grumpty and his warrior three were gradually making their way to one of the few huts still left standing. His chains were bloody from fighting, and some matted fur was trapped in one of the links. All of a sudden, they found their way blocked by the She-Wolf and three other wolves. A breeze whipped up and a pinecone danced across the forest floor between them.

The wind rattled the chains that the elves were carrying, and the She-Wolf observed them for a moment before returning her gaze to Grumpty. Barkle shivered and eyed the four wolves standing opposite them.

The She-Wolf was the largest and had a tougher more battle-hardened look to her, but the other wolves didn't exactly look tame in comparison. Although limited, the four elves had experienced some fighting from their previous adventures. It had been enough to help them make it this far, but even though the numbers were matched, Barkle doubted they stood a chance against these wolves.

Despite this, the four elves stood four abreast, gripping their chains in their hands tightly. It felt somehow appropriate to use the tools of their incarceration as weapons. The She-Wolf sniggerd, and the wolves either side of her joined in. Nut swallowed hard as he gazed at the wolf standing opposite him. It was a big bruiser of an animal with a prominent forehead and mean eyes.

The two lines of warriors stood facing each other for a moment. Around them the dwarves were doing their best to beat down the wolves. Despite their best efforts it looked like they were struggling. Like the elves, the dwarves had not been in battle for many years.

Although they continued to practice and train back in the mountains, their lack of first-hand experience was painfully apparent. Not to mention that the wolves were using incredibly dirty and underhand tactics to best their opponents. Azral wanted to shout out for help, but he knew it was futile. The dwarves who were nearby were too occupied with surviving themselves to worry about a handful of elves. The She-Wolf narrowed her eyes and then gave a sudden gruff growl.

The four wolves darted forwards. Grumpty was terrified but adrenaline was coursing through his veins. He let out a war cry and also charged forwards. His friends joined in and soon the two lines of foes were dashing towards one another, the wolves growling and the elves shouting.

The She-Wolf was about a metre away from Grumpty, close enough for him to see the ferocious glint in her eye, when several shadows passed over them. The She-Wolf, who was slightly further ahead than the rest of the pack, leapt into the air. Grumpty ran to meet her, swinging his chain wildly in front of him.

There was a shrill cry and Mother Owl appeared and slammed into the She-Wolf, where she began attacking her repeatedly with her talons. Three more owls swooped down, pecking and slashing at the other wolves feriously.

The four elves watched on stunned, as the wolves turned on the owls and began jumping up, teeth bared. But the owls were too agile, and dodged nimbly out of the way, then back up into the air before dive bombing back down again for another aerial attack.

'Save the others. We will hold them off,' Mother Owl shouted, catching sight of an awestruck Grumpty.

Grumpty didn't want to leave the owls to deal with the wolves alone, but he knew arguing with Mother Owl was pointless. With the wolves distracted; the elves quickly made tracks. The She-Wolf caught sight of the escaping elves and went to pursue. The animal let out a yelp of pain and glanced round.

Mother Owl had pinned her tail to the ground in her large talons. The She-Wolf thrashed furiously and freed herself from the owl's hold. She turned to face Mother Owl. It was time to teach the stupid bird a lesson, she thought to herself.

As the four elves sprinted towards the huts they could hear the hoots and calls of the flying owls, who zoomed and zipped high above, until they selected their targets and dived in for the attack. Seeing the wolves suddenly on the back foot, the dwarves who were still standing fought back with renewed strength.

Grumpty and his friends reached the nearest hut and briefly took a moment to catch their breath. Barkle was covered in sweat, the hair under his moleskin hat dripping onto his jacket. Nut was doubled over and wheezing, and Azral had dispatched of his hat and coat, in a bid to cool himself down.

'You and Nut check this and the other huts Barkle and I will check the church,' Grumpty instructed, when he had caught his breath.

Nut nodded and wiped the moisture from his brow. Azral was frowning hard.

'Barkle had a weapon.'

Grumpty looked at Barkle.

'A weapon,' he asked. Where?'

Barkle, red faced and exhasperated, shrugged his shoulders and Azral thumped the side of the hut in frustration. Grumpty placed a consoling hand on his shoulder.

'It's okay, stick to the plan. The church is the biggest place so it could well be in there. Keep an eye out when searching the huts.'

Azral nodded and elbowing Nut, ducked inside the hut. Nut, who looked like he was going to pass out, puffed out his cheeks before entering the hut himself.

'Come on Barkle,' Grumpty said and the two set off towards the church.

Three prisoner elves were huddled in the corner of the first hut, too scared to go anywhere. No wolves or dwarves were in sight and Azral and Nut presumed they had abandoned their posts to join in the fighting. The prisoner elves looked exhausted but otherwise unharmed. At first, they wouldn't move, so Nut sat down beside them and with a calm and relaxing voice tried to gently persuade them to leave the hut for the safety of the trees.

Azral meanwhile stood by the hut entrance, keeping an eye on things outside. The wolves, although now on the back-foot, fought on defiantly. Not only was the battle deeply personal, but they really couldn't afford to lose to the elves a second time. The humiliation would be too much to bear.

A few times fighting dwarves, owls and wolves drew dangerously close to the hut they were in. Azral glanced at Nut impatiently but didn't say anything. The prisoner elves were easily spooked, and he didn't want to undo all his friend's hard work.

Eventually Nut managed to convince them to leave, but only under one condition, that Nut would lead them to safety. Azral didn't think splitting up was a good idea, but he could see that it was clearly the only way the prisoner elves were going to agree to leave.

So, exiting the hut the two friends parted ways, Nut heading out of the village with the rescued elves, and Azral on to the next hut. Azral had nearly reached the second hut when a wolf sprang out of nowhere and clamped its teeth around his arm.

He let out a howl of pain and started whipping the beast with his chain. The chain drew blood and so did the wolf's teeth but still the animal didn't let go. A big boot swung up into the wolf's midriff and the animal released its hold, crumpling to the ground.

An imposing dwarf moved to stand over the felled animal and rested her long blade against the wolf's throat. She glanced at Azral, who had turned ghostly white and was clutching his blood drenched arm.

'Wrap something round that sharpish to stop the blood loss,' the dwarf advised.

Feeling decidedly woozy, Azral ripped off a section of his hemp shirt and tied it tightly around his arm. He had lost enough blood to know that it would only serve to sustain him for so long. Head swimming and arm throbbing, Azral gritted his teeth and pushed on.

The blood was hot and sticky and looking at the wound made him instantly queasy. The wounded elf managed to reach the hut but was overcome by nausea as he passed through the door flap. He fell over the threshold and hit the floor, already unconscious.

Barkle and Grumpty had been more fortunate in their endeavours. The inventor wasn't a particularly good fighter, but he had good reflexes. Grumpty was not an experienced fighter either, but there was a toughness to him, and the two managed to fend off any attackers on the way.

The owls had been a big help and the dwarves seemed to have gotten a second wind as a result of their arrival. The two elves were a little surprised that the religious building had remained standing. While the doors had been broken down and the surrounding graveyard desecrated, the building itself appeared unharmed.

Grumpty wasn't a firm believer but at this particular moment he prayed dearly that Barkle's weapon was inside, and more importantly that the elves were still alive. A few dead dwarves and wolves lay in the graveyard outside the church. It felt unnatural to Barkle.

Bodies obviously belonged in graveyards, but he preferred them to be underground, as opposed to on top of it. The other thing that seemed odd was that this part of the village was eerily quiet. Everywhere else the sounds of fighting could be heard, but in the churchyard, there was no noise. The birdsong that usually filled the trees had vanished.

Barkle and Grumpty made their way gingerly around the bodies and into the church. Although they had seen enough bodies to last a lifetime in an incredibly short space of time, it had the same effect every time. Whereas the outside of the church had remained fairly intact, the inside was the complete opposite.

Most of the wooden benches that lined either side of the

grand building had been knocked over, and more dead wolves and dwarves lay next to them or sprawled awkwardly on top. Grumpty was dismayed to see a few fallen elves here and there as well. His foot connected with one of the empty dwarf helmets and it rolled across the wooden floorboards, rattling loudly.

There was a sudden movement from somewhere at the back of church, and something large and dark shot towards him. It landed over his head, wrapping itself tightly around his body. The force of the object had knocked Grumpty off balance, and he fell to the ground with a deep grunt.

For a split second he began to panic, as he feared he had been trapped in a massive spider's web. But the arachnids were a myth, a folk-tale told by the elders around the fire at night to scare the young 'uns. Besides, even if they did exist, they lived well beyond Finhorn Forest and past the mountains. Barkle's face suddenly loomed into sight above him. He was smiling.

'Don't worry, it's just Ogle and some of the others.'

Calming himself down, Grumpty inspected his restraints and realised it was a large rope net as opposed to a spider's web. If it was Ogle, then why on earth had he thrown this strange net over him, Grumpty thought to himself.

'Hi Grumpty,' said Ogle, appearing beside Barkle and regarding the small captured elf with a guilty look.

'While it is good to see you Ogle, would you mind getting me out of this blasted net?' Grumpty replied calmly, but his voice had a hint of anger to it.

The two elves set about cutting the ropes, much to Grumpty's relief. The rope was coarse and dug into his skin and scratched his already injured face. It took a while, but eventually enough of the rope sections were hacked away and Grumpty was able to wriggle free from the rope prison. He got to his feet tutting and massaged his tender arms and hands.

'Why on earth did you do....' he began, but was interrupted when Ogle embraced him in a tight hug.

All the irritation and disappointment at Ogle's mistake suddenly faded away and Grumpty relaxed for the first time all day, allowing himself a moment to just enjoy the heartfelt hug thrust upon him. When the two finally stepped away from each other, Grumpty realised there were tears on Ogle's face.

'What's wrong?' he asked, putting a hand on his friend's shoulder.

'Father Mugleaf,' he said in a low voice and the words seemed to trap in his throat for a moment. 'He... didn't make it.'

Grumpty had been hit hard a few times today but nothing had caused as much impact as the news Ogle had just revealed. Not saying anything, Grumpty moved over to one of the few remaining pews and perched on the end. Ogle went to follow but Barkle stopped him.

'Give him a moment lad.'

Ogle nodded and wiped his tear stained face. Barkle felt a tug on his moleskin tunic and glanced down. A young elf was looking up at him. In his other hand he was holding the inventor's crossbow and struggling to lift the big contraption. Barkle knelt down, ruffled the young elf's brown hair and took the crossbow from him.

'Thank you little one.'

He stood up. A small gaggle of elves were watching him and Ogle a little way away. One of them, a female elf with frizzy brown hair, was gesticulating towards the young elf, who gave Barkle a warm smile, before returning to his mother. The assembled elves were a mixture of ages and one or two of them stood with the aid of makeshift crutches. A few others had bandages wrapped around their heads and arms.

'Is this all there is?' Barkle said grimly.

'Here...yes,' Ogle replied. 'We held our own but not all of us made it. If it hadn't been for your crossbow, things could have been a lot worse,' he said appreciatively.

Barkle looked around. Indeed a few of the wolves had been captured by the nets. They weren't moving and an uncomfortable pang of guilt gripped him. He preferred that it had been wolves rather than elves, but there was the horrible feeling that his invention had become a weapon of destruction.

Whether purposefully or not, Barkle had played his part in the taking of lives. This was why the elves had laid down their weapons and vowed to be a peaceful race all those years ago. War was a truly terrible thing and Barkle wasn't sure he was ever going to be able to forget what he had seen here today.

~~~

The Dwarf Queen and the Haggard Wolf were still knee deep in their grudge match. Both bore battle wounds, but fought on despite their afflictions. A few of the Haggard Wolf's sharp teeth had been knocked out and one of his eyes was closing up. The Dwarf Queen was missing two of her fingers and the armour plating that hadn't been torn off was heavily dented and scratched. They were both limping and exhausted from the fight.

With a great groan the Dwarf Queen surged forwards, axe raised above her head. She swung it down fast and hard. The Haggard Wolf managed to roll out the way in time and jumped back up, ready to retaliate. The Dwarf Queen had made a terrible judgement of error. She had applied so much force into her swing that the axe was now stuck in the ground.

Seeing her attempting desperately to wrench it free, the Haggard Wolf saw an opportunity to attack. He leapt onto the Dwarf Queen's back and started biting and clawing at her helmet. If he could prize the heavy piece of armour off the Dwarf Queen's head, her face would be exposed.

She roared in surprise and reached behind her, trying to grab the furry beast, but the Haggard Wolf was agile and wouldn't stop moving. Whenever she tried to grab him, he would snap and bite at her exposed hands. Hefting herself onto to her feet she windmilled around wildly, trying to detach the infernal animal.

She crashed through the village looking for a wall, building or tree to slam the wolf against. But most of the huts were destroyed and the trees were too far away. The Dwarf Queen's helmet was starting to detach itself from the top of her head and she knew she had to get rid of the Haggard Wolf soon.

His tail brushed against her face and she had a sudden idea.

Seizing hold of its fluffy end, she yanked it hard. The Haggard Wolf screamed in alarm and slackened his grip.

The Dwarf Queen used all of her remaining strength and threw the animal off. The Haggard Wolf landed awkwardly on the broken timbers of one of the huts and let out an almighty howl, as his already injured leg made a horrible snapping sound. He lay there still for a moment and the Dwarf Queen presumed he had given up. But then, astonishingly, the Haggard Wolf began to drag himself over the rubble towards her. As much as the Dwarf Queen disliked the animal for his underhand tactics and general untrustworthiness, she had to admire his resilience.

The Haggard Wolf stood up, his other three legs shaking precariously as they had to take the weight of his body from his broken one. It hung limply at the back and the Haggard Wolf wobbled a few times, almost losing balance. But he remained upright and regarded the Dwarf Queen cruelly. She was under the impression that dwarves had a bad reputation for vengeance, but that seemed to pale somewhat compared to wolves.

'Give up, you have lost,' she said, gesturing around the half-demolished village.

Although the wolves still fought on defiantly, they were being slowly pushed back. The owls were doing a tremendous job of distracting and infuriating the four-legged animals. This allowed the dwarves to rush in and catch them off guard. Even the more sly and tactical animals who had cottoned on to this were failing to make a difference.

They were simply outnumbered. The Haggard Wolf felt truly cursed. Things were supposed to have been different this time, he thought to himself. They had started off with the greater force and yet the tables had been completely turned.

He limped towards the Dwarf Queen. There was no turning back now. The Haggard Wolf had already lost one battle and the shame had almost been too much. The same would not happen again. He had made his decision. To see his mission through to the end, whatever the outcome. Seeing him approach the Dwarf Queen started stripping off her armour. A nearby dwarf rushed forwards, confused as to her actions but she waved him away. The Haggard Wolf was at a disadvantage and she wasn't willing to strike an enemy down unfairly.

The Haggard Wolf went to attack but the movement was clumsy and slow. The Dwarf Queen sidestepped out of the way easily and punched him on the side of his head with a meaty fist, the Haggard Wolf staggered sideways, and his legs gave way. He crashed to the ground. The dwarves and wolves were gradually giving up on their fights, their attention becoming drawn to their leader's scuffle, knowing the outcome of this encounter would determine what happened next.

The Haggard Wolf gritted his teeth and tried with all his might to get to his feet. There was no strength left in his body and the large wolf collapsed to the ground once more, where he lay panting and defeated. There was a brief silence, as the spectators waited to make sure the Haggard Wolf wasn't going to try again. But the wolf was spent, and he dug his face into the ground, trying to hide the tears of shame and humiliation welling up in his eyes.

A few of the dwarves and elves looked at each other for confirmation, then a massive cheer rose up. The owls circling above hooted triumphantly, as the She-Wolf, flanked by two digger wolves, moved over to retrieve their defeated leader.

The Dwarf Queen glanced wearily around the village and smiled, as dwarves and elves stood side by side raising their weapons in the air victoriously. She caught sight of Grumpty, and a group of elves standing a little way away. He had a gash on his forehead and looked a little bruised and battered, but seemed okay apart from that. They locked eyes and nodded at one another.

Sighing deeply, the Dwarf Queen sat down heavily on the grass and watched the wolves slowly leave the village. The sun broke through the clouds and she felt its warm rays wash over her. The Dwarf Queen closed her eyes and drank in its warmth.

CHAPTER 7:
THE DEAL

It was a solemn day following the battle with the wolves. The dead were buried, and a ceremony was held for the fallen. Although they had both fought alongside each other, the dwarves held a separate vigil just outside the village. Grumpty had invited them to partake in a joint vigil for the dead, but the Dwarf Queen had politely declined.

Many of the elves felt the dwarves were still responsible for what had happened. Knowing it wasn't entirely untrue, the Dwarf Queen had chosen to carry out their burial nearby, but out of sight. Ogle and Nut deeply loathed the lingering presence of the dwarves and wished they would just leave.

Grumpty could understand their hatred but didn't have the energy to join in. They had survived and that was the important thing. Yes, the dwarves had done them a disservice by attacking in the first place, but what was done was done. In the end they had made the right decision and corrected their mistake, but it wasn't just a simple case of them leaving.

Like it or not the dwarves had come to the village in search of new territory to occupy. Grumpty wasn't willing to hand over control and so discussions would have to be made. An agreement between the two races needed to be established before they could move forward. For the time being though, it was important to take a moment and pay their respects to the brave elves and dwarves that had died on the battlefield.

Grumpty couldn't help but shed some tears at the ceremony

especially when Father Mugleaf was mentioned. He had remarked to Barkle and Ogle in the church that he felt guilty and he should have done more to the protect the village. His two friends had insisted it was not the case and that Mugleaf was just an unfortunate casualty of war, as were the other fallen elves. Grumpty knew Barkle and Ogle were right, but that didn't stop the thoughts from playing around in his head.

After a respectful and contemplative ceremony some emotional but serene music was played by some of the elves. The songs rang through the clearing and the owls, who had returned to their post in the trees, sat quietly and appreciated the melodies.

Mother Owl had lost her scout to the battle and a few others had been injured, but she felt extremely lucky that they had not suffered more losses. The music even carried as far as to where the dwarves had set up camp, a little further into the trees. Dwarves had a great affinity for music as well as elves, but it was never used for the passing of kin.

The ceremonies were short and to the point. Respect and tribute were paid and that was that. But listening to the enchanting music emanating from the village, the Dwarf Queen couldn't help but wonder if her own burial traditions were missing something. She had already changed so much since her time as ruler, but it still felt like a lot of the dwarven culture and practices were still entrenched in the past.

When male dwarves had still been in charge it was all about repressing the emotions, pushing down any feelings as it was seen as a weakness, but they were wrong. Emotion was the key to success. If she had ignored her feelings about the wolves, her race would have been responsible for wiping out an elven community who had done nothing wrong.

Her elder advisor probably hated the idea of more change, as she was a fervent believer in tradition, but it was not her decision to make. The Dwarf Queen was the leader and she aimed to change things for the better while she was still in power.

After the dwarven ceremony, many of them set about establishing a camp. The elves still had the task of rebuilding the village and it would take a lot of time, considering the extent of the damage. While the dwarves started constructing dens, collecting firewood and seeing to their injuries, the Dwarf Queen went for a walk by herself.

She needed time to think about the next move. During the battle, the dwarves and elves had formed a temporary alliance of sorts, but it was clear, now that the bloodshed was over, that the elves wanted nothing further to do with the dwarves. The Dwarf Queen also had to consider her own people.

They supported her loyally and agreed that avoiding violence was always preferable. However, they had marched a fair way from the mountains and had lost kin and friends along the way. She knew that they would not be happy to leave empty handed. It could certainly threaten her tenure as Queen.

If a better suited dwarf would serve as her replacement, then maybe she would have considered it. But unfortunately, the other candidates vying for her throne were either too traditional or alternatively too radical.

It was a surprisingly pleasant walk through the trees and the Dwarf Queen inhaled deeply, imbibing the earthy smells of the woods around her. Birdsong had returned to the canopy above and it made her both calm and mournful. The fact that life carried on regardless could be seen as almost insincere from a particular perspective. On the other hand, it could be viewed that with every end there comes a new beginning. A turning over of a new leaf.

The Dwarf Queen stopped at a fallen log and sat down on the ground resting her back against the large solid trunk. Every part of her body ached and the various injuries she had suffered hurt like mad. Her body was putting all of its work and energy into repairing itself and that left the Dwarf Queen feeling extremely drained.

Part of the pain and fatigue lay in the fact that it was the first time she had allowed herself to rest. When in the company of the other dwarves she had kept up appearances, trying to remain strong and set an example. But now, hidden behind a log away from the rest of the company, she could allow it all to come out.

A few tears escaped as she sat slumped ungainly against the

fallen tree. It wasn't that she was particularly upset. The deaths of some of her fellow dwarves had been deeply sad, but it hadn't really sunk in yet. The tears came from absolute exhaustion more than anything.

Wiping at her slightly wet face with one of her large arms, she started laughing. It came out of nowhere and soon a big grin had spread across her face. The sun shining through the canopy above was brilliant and it fell on the forest floor in a beautiful dappled effect.

The Dwarf Queen had spent her entire life in the mountains and been forbidden to go outside as a young dwarf. By the time she was old enough to consider it, she was crowned the new Dwarf Queen following her older sister's untimely death, due to illness. After her coronation there was no time to be given to any thoughts of venturing outside the mountain.

At first, she hadn't been interested in the royal position thrust upon her. However, it had soon become clear that change could be made, and progression achieved. As ideas and concepts had begun to take hold, the desire to explore the world had become lost to matters of the State.

It was only now, sitting in the serene picturesque forest that the Dwarf Queen realised what she had been missing. Everywhere she looked there was something to marvel at. Be it the lush flora that surrounded her, or the little creatures that scurried up and down the trees and across the forest floor.

Impressively, the dwarves had excelled in craftsmanship and engineering, not to mention remoulding and heavily improving their society, but the mountains were dark and cold. Unlike the autumnal forest, which was a rich and vibrant mix of greens and browns.

A cloud passed overhead, and the forest turned a darker shade all of a sudden. The Dwarf Queen's smile faded from her face. She suddenly appeared serious; her bushy eyebrows furrowed in a deep frown. But it wasn't a look of anger or concern, more that she was thinking about something very hard. An idea was coming together in her mind. A possible solution to the problems the dwarves and the elves both faced. The cogs were beginning to turn, despite how seized up they felt.

~~~

Usually after a burial, the elves would have a wake, but they were never solemn affairs. Grief was expressed at the ceremony itself. However, the elves did not want to fixate on the sadness. Instead, they chose to honour and celebrate the life of the fallen by having a party. Tales would be told; music would be played, and acorn wine would be poured.

It was traditional and brought everyone closer together at a time of strife and turmoil. Unfortunately, the village was in a state and a clear up was the first priority. A wake would eventually be held, but after their homes had been repaired and made safe.

Grumpty was actually grateful for the work. Although all his energy was spent, the small elf's brain had gone into overdrive. Keeping himself busy was a much-needed distraction from the multitude of thoughts running around his mind. His face stung badly from the vicious slashes given to him by the Haggard Wolf.

He had been routinely applying the strange balm the Dwarf Queen had given him. It helped eased the pain, but the biggest scars Grumpty was suffering from were on the inside. The small elf had lost people before but Mugleaf's passing had changed him. It wasn't even grief or sadness anymore, just a hollow emptiness that seemed to consume him.

Nut and Ogle had tried talking to him on a number of occasions, and although he had responded, his answers were vague, and it was evident that the small elf wasn't really paying attention. In the end they had left him alone and gone to another part of the village that was in need of repairing.

It was hard to know where to start, as there wasn't really anywhere that hadn't been partly or completely demolished. Ideally, they should have organised specific groups with set jobs in certain areas. But for once Grumpty didn't step up as leader and so everyone ended up mucking in wherever was needed.

Mother Owl had stopped by and spoken briefly with Grumpty. She was going to do a sweep of some of the further parts of the forest, to make sure there were no lingering threats still present. Grumpty didn't think it was likely that the wolves would return but he didn't say so. He knew that it was more about Mother Owl stretching her wings and clearing her mind.

The battle had taken its toll on all the races and each had their own way of dealing with it. For the elves it was restoring normality to their village, and for the owls it was taking to the skies and putting distance between them and the scene of the conflict.

Ogle and Nut were moving a section of demolished roof and some wooden beams onto a nearby cart, when one of the elves stopped his work and pointed towards the trees. The dwarves were making their way into the village from the treeline. The Dwarf Queen was at the head of the procession and limping slightly, but her face only showed mild discomfort.

They were a tough bunch, Nut thought to himself. No one protested the dwarven arrival, but the elves looked at them warily. Others were muttering under their breath to one another. Ogle gripped the piece of wood he was carrying a little tighter. The Dwarf Queen gestured with her arms and the dwarves following her began to break off in different directions.

One of them approached Ogle and Nut and they tensed themselves ready for trouble, but the dwarf gave them an awkward smile, picked up a large and heavy part of the roof and carried it over to the cart. Nut relaxed, as did several other elves scattered around the village and jumped back into his work once more.

Grumpty was sifting through the wreckage of one of the elven barricades, when the broad shadow of the Dwarf Queen fell across him. He sighed, threw down the section of crate he was holding and rose to his feet.

'How are your battle wounds holding up?' she said, gesturing at his face.

'Still sore and it hurts when I smile. Luckily, I'm not in the mood for smiling anyway,' he said bitterly.

The Dwarf Queen lowered her head shamefully.

'I'm sorry I had a hand in this. If I had known...'

Grumpty held up a hand, cutting her off.

'It is done. Besides, you didn't know.'

The Dwarf Queen studied the small elf for a moment. He had changed. While his compassion and forgiveness seemed genuine, there was something different about him. Before he had come across as strong, brave and a little bull-headed. There had also been a natural leader like quality to him despite his small statue.

That was why the Dwarf Queen had entertained talking to him in the first place. Like herself, Grumpty seemed born to lead, but that charisma and passion was gone now. An air of despondency lingered over Grumpty, like an ominous black cloud. The elf looked the same, but there was a cold detachment in his eyes. Even talking to him, the Dwarf Queen felt like it was falling on deaf ears.

'What are they doing here?' shouted an angry voice behind them.

The Dwarf Queen and Grumpty looked round. Ogle was storming towards them, a look of utter contempt on his face. Grumpty sighed heavily and went to speak, but Ogle beat him to it.

'Haven't they done enough damage?'

'Which is why we want to help you. Make things right,' the Dwarf Queen said calmly.

Ogle snorted with indignation.

'You could help by leaving us alone,' Ogle snorted with indignation. 'We don't need you.'

The Dwarf Queen glanced around. Her dwarves were carrying the same size and weight of debris as the elves, but it only took one of them. The elves on the other hand needed at least two or three of them to lift and transport the objects.

'It certainly looks like you could use the help.'

Ogle moved in close to the Dwarf Queen, and for a moment she thought he was going to swing a punch. Not that it fazed her much. Instead, Ogle jabbed a finger at her.

'I'm not scared of you and I'm not buying this act of yours.'

Grumpty slid in between them and guided Ogle's arm back down to his side. His friend let him, but continued to eye the

Dwarf Queen furiously.

'I've got this under control Ogle. We are going to have a discussion and straighten this whole thing out, but for the time being I need you to help the others rebuild. The dwarves won't bother you if you don't bother them, right?' he said, glancing at the Dwarf Queen for confirmation.

'Absolutely,' she responded confidently.

Ogle stared at her for a moment, his eyebrows still quivering with anger. Then he looked at Grumpty, who put a hand on his friend's shoulder and said,

'Trust me.'

Ogle chewed his lip pensively for a moment, then nodded, untensing his shoulders. He gave the Dwarf Queen one last look of disgust and turned to leave. Grumpty watched him walking away for a moment before turning around.

'He clearly doesn't like me,' the Dwarf Queen remarked.

'Can you blame him?' Grumpy said bluntly.

She shook her head and glanced around. The elves and dwarves were hard at work clearing away the demolished huts, but they kept looking over at the two leaders curiously.

'Is there somewhere private we can talk?'

'I know a place,' Grumpty said.

~~~

The Dwarf Queen slipped and stumbled down the hill, finding it difficult to keep balanced on the gradient. It didn't help that her war wounds were still fresh and her body stiff.

'Not much further now,' Grumpty said over his shoulder.

The small elf didn't seem to be struggling half as much as the Dwarf Queen. He was light footed and nimble despite his injuries and knew how to effectively navigate the woods. The Dwarf Queen on the other hand, suffered from a combination of being too heavy, off balanced due to her injuries and unfamiliar with the terrain.

She wondered if the route was a deliberate decision on Grumpty's part to get back at her. The birds that tweeted in the trees above no longer soothed the Dwarf Queen, but instead sounded like they were taunting her cruelly. Grumpty reached the bottom of the hill and disappeared through a screen of trees. The Dwarf Queen hoped it wasn't his idea of a joke.

She cursed, grabbing hold of a tree trunk to stop herself slipping on some loose undergrowth. Her recent love and admiration of the forest had turned into one of deep loathing. It felt like nature had turned against her. If it wasn't the mocking birds, it was the unpredictable loose soil and roots. In her haste to reach the base of the slope, she sped up slightly and lost her balance.

Grumpty was inspecting Barkle's alarm contraption when the Dwarf Queen crashed through the trees and fell to her knees in the clearing. He moved to help her up, but she flapped him away, getting to her feet with a deep groan. Her face had turned a bright shade of red and she was breathing heavily.

'You know it doesn't make you weak asking for help,' Grumpty said casually.

The Dwarf Queen glared at him hard for a moment, then to Grumpty's surprise her expression suddenly softened.

'Force of habit,' she said and moved over to a nearby rock and lowered herself carefully onto it.

'I was raised to be strong and not rely on anyone but myself.'

'Must have been tough for you,' Grumpty said compassionately.

The Dwarf Queen gave a low grunt in response and checked her wounds to make sure none had reopened. Fortunately, they had not, but her body was making it clear that it wasn't prepared for it to happen again. Grumpty watched her silently. The two locked eyes. It was as if the elf was expecting her to say something.

'What's that?' she said, gesturing at Barkle's invention.

It was obvious that the Dwarf Queen was trying to change the subject. Grumpty understood that. Ogle and Nut had been trying to get him to talk all morning, but he didn't want to talk about it. The wounds were still too fresh. In time it would be dealt with, but not now. Not while there was so much left to do. If Grumpty started talking, he was afraid he wouldn't be able to stop.

'It's an alarm system.'

The Dwarf Queen nodded slowly, looking a little perplexed.

'Not a very good one then.'

Grumpty rested a hand on top of the mechanism.

'I think Barkle may have got the calculations wrong with the range of the device.'

'Perhaps it would work better if it wasn't at the bottom of a hill,' the Dwarf Queen pointed out.

Grumpty looked at her sharply and she simply shrugged in response.

'Just saying.'

'Maybe you're right,' Grumpty said with a belated sigh.

He seemed distracted and was drumming his fingertips on the contraption impatiently.

'So, this little problem of ours. I think I may have a solution,' the Dwarf Queen said, folding her large arms.

Grumpty stopped drumming and looked directly at her. For the first time since they had started talking, he actually looked like he was paying attention. Thuds and rumbles carried down the hill to them from the village. It was slightly muffled from here, but Grumpty could tell the noise was from the carts being moved around.

'How well do you know the forest?' the Dwarf Queen asked.

Grumpty frowned. He had spent most of his childhood in the safe confines of the village. But ever since he had left on his first adventure, his knowledge of the area had grown considerably. It had further developed through his time spent with the owls.

'I have a pretty good knowledge of the forest but Azral is the elf you want to speak to.'

The Dwarf Queen nodded.

'How is your friend by the way?'

'He lost a lot of blood, but he will pull through. Barkle has been by his side and says he is slowly on the mend,' Grumpty said, not knowing how to feel about the Dwarf Queen asking after an elf.

'That's good,' she said awkwardly, before returning to the matter in hand.

'I have an idea. A deal if you like, that I think will work for both of us.'

Grumpty said nothing but continued to look intrigued. Truthfully, he just wanted the Dwarf Queen to spit it out. The sooner this whole mess was sorted out the better.

'I want to form an alliance with the elves,' she said after a moment's brief contemplation.

Grumpty took a while to process what she had said and strolled back and forth in front of her, stroking his chin thoughtfully. The Dwarf Queen felt a stabbing jolt of pain from the wound in her abdomen and readjusted herself on the stone.

'There not going to like it,' Grumpty said eventually.

'Just listen to my proposal,' the Dwarf Queen said, looking to the small elf for confirmation.

He sat down on the grass in front of her and looked at her fixedly. The Dwarf Queen took that to mean he was happy for her to go on.

'We were promised a settlement by the wolves but if we had known the truth earlier the negotiations would have never been entertained in the first place. But the point still stands, and my people won't accept returning home empty handed. Not when their sisters have given their lives to the cause.'

Grumpty said nothing. His head was cocked to one side and he was mulling over what she was saying.

'What if you were to help us find a new settlement. That way you can retain control of your village and we get what we came for,' the Dwarf Queen put forth.

Grumpty sat up intrigued and his eyes seemed a bit more alive for a moment.

'You're saying you will leave us alone if we help you find somewhere else to occupy?'

The Dwarf Queen nodded but held up a finger.

'However, we want to establish trade between your village and wherever we settle.'

'Trade?' Grumpty said surprised.

He had not been expecting that, but it made sense. The

dwarves had wealth and rich materials mined from the mountains, but in order to build a sustainable community in Finhorn Forest they would need materials and provisions that only the elves possessed. The Dwarf Queen nodded enthusiastically; a hopeful gleam in her eyes.

'And what would we get in return?' Grumpty queried. 'I don't mean to be so blunt but if I am taking a proposal back to my people, I need a good reason to convince them.'

The Dwarf Queen thought for a moment and then replied,

'As well as getting access to some of our finest materials, armours and weaponry, we are willing to act as your war allies.'

Grumpty looked a little confused so the Dwarf Queen further elaborated.

'The wolves seem to have a personal vendetta against you and your people. Needless to say, that is probably the case for us as well. If they do choose to attack you again, we will come to your aid. Unless of course you prefer to deal with them by yourselves.'

'No no... the help would be much appreciated,' Grumpty said a little too quickly.

Realising that he must have sounded desperate, Grumpty quickly recomposed himself. The Dwarf Queen was observing him shrewdly.

'And what do your people think of this idea,' Grumpty said, trying to come across professional once more.

'They are in agreement. Question is, will your people be?' the Dwarf Queen said, clasping her hands together tightly.

~~~

When they got back to the village, it was clear that both the elves and dwarves had been hard at work. A lot of rebuilding and repairing was still to be done, but the majority of the debris had been carted away. A few of the elves and dwarves were actually talking to one another as they worked. Most still gave each other a wide berth, and Ogle kept glancing at the dwarf helping him suspiciously.

'It will be better if I talk to them alone about this matter. Otherwise it might get a little heated,' Grumpty explained.

'Of course, but I think you might have your work cut out,' the Dwarf Queen said, eyeing Ogle ruefully.

The Dwarf Queen moved off, signalling at the other dwarves as she passed through the village. They gratefully finished what they were doing and fell in behind her. Both the elves and dwarves looked tired and were sweating heavily. The ceremonies had been a bit of a reprieve after the intense battle but neither race had been allowed suitable time to recover.

Some of the elves were so spent that they sat down exactly where they had been standing. Others went off in search of food and water, as well as a place to lie down for a while. Grumpty moved over to Ogle and Nut. Nut looked extremely weary but was looking round at the village proudly.

'We've done a fine job Grumpty.'

'I can see that,' Grumpty said, smiling at his friend.

'Is that it then? They do a few hours work and then leave us to do the rest?' Ogle said indignantly.

Grumpty rolled his eyes at Nut, who grinned. The small elf seemed a bit more like himself and the older elf was relieved. He did not like to see his friend so downtrodden and morose.

'You said that you didn't want them interfering in the first place,' Grumpty pointed out.

Ogle gave an uncomfortable shrug.

'Yeah well that was before. This mess is partly their fault, so it is only right they help clear it up.'

Grumpty gave his friend an encouraging albeit condescending nod of agreement.

'I need you to gather up all the elves and get them to assemble at the mossy stone. Rope Barkle into helping you if necessary.'

'What's going on Grumpty?' Nut asked puzzled.

'You'll find out soon enough,' Grumpty said mysteriously.

~~~

The gathered elves stood huddled around the mossy stone, muttering and chatting noisily to one another. Ogle, and Nut were stood at the front. Unlike the others they were quiet and watching the mossy stone, waiting for their friend to appear. A breeze rose up and some of the attending elves shivered, hugging their mole-skin jackets closer to themselves.

Someone gasped in surprise and pointed to the stone. Grumpty had appeared and was standing with his hands on his hips, legs spread in a wide stance. With the wind ruffling his hair he looked very windswept and adventurous. It was Ogle's turn to roll his eyes.

'Thank you for your patience,' Grumpty announced loudly to the crowd.

A deep hush descended over the elves and they waited eagerly for him to continue. As a child Grumpty had never been a very confident elf, due to little encouragement from his parents, especially his father, intense bullying and never being listened to. However, since travelling beyond the village, living with the owls and getting into a few hairy situations, Grumpty found public speaking surprisingly easy.

'I know it has been hard accepting help from the dwarves after they were originally allied with the wolves. But after discussing the matter with the Dwarf Queen, I think we have come to a solution that is fair.'

He paused for dramatic effect. Everyone was hanging on his words and all eyes were focused his way. Grumpty took a deep breath and cast his eyes over the crowd. A swell of pride rose within him. Even after all the devastation and disaster caused by the wolves they were still willing to hear him out.

He proceeded to outline the proposal, slightly repeating and rephrasing the words the Dwarf Queen had said to him previously. Nobody interrupted or raised their hands but continued to wait patiently until Grumpty had finished giving his speech. When the small elf had concluded his announcement, he eyed the crowd hopefully, despite feeling more than a little apprehensive.

'Are there any questions or is everyone okay with this suggestion?'

The elves glanced at each other and a few of them shrugged nonchalantly. Grumpty was taken aback. He thought a handful of them would have resisted for sure. Glancing at Ogle he expected his friend to be scowling or shaking his head disapprovingly, but the elf didn't seem perturbed in the slightness. If anything, Ogle looked a little pleased.

'...excellent, I will tell the Dwarf Queen right away. Thank you everyone for being so understanding,' Grumpty said, still reeling from the lack of resistance.

He went to climb down but paused when the sound of clapping made him look round. A few others joined in and soon the whole crowd was applauding. Grumpty beamed at the celebrating spectators and felt a surge of warmth spread through him.

~~~

After he had stopped briefly by the Dwarf Queen's camp to let her know the good news, Grumpty had paid Azral a visit. He was tucked up in bed in one of the few huts that had managed to avoid being destroyed in the fighting. Barkle was sat in a chair next to his bed, fiddling with yet another contraption, when Grumpty ducked inside the hut. Azral was asleep. He looked very pale and clammy and somehow frailer than usual.

'Don't you ever stop working?' Grumpty said, with an amused curl of the lip.

Barkle, who was frowning hard at the gadget in his hands, looked up and chuckled. There was a low groan and Azral opened his eyes. Barkle climbed out of the chair and motioned for Grumpty to sit in it.

'My dear friend,' the small elf said softly, as he slid into the chair. 'How are you feeling?'

'Oh, you know, full of the joys of spring...except its autumn,' he said croakily and gave a weak smile.

Grumpty looked kindly upon his friend and gave Azral's hand a tight squeeze. The elf grimaced a little.

'Not that arm, it's still tender.'

'Sorry, that was silly of me,' Grumpty said, releasing his hold quickly.

Azral yawned and tried to widen his sleepy eyes. It was hard to stay awake when he was constantly assailed by such heavy waves of tiredness.

'Did we win?'

'Yes, we won,' Grumpty said with a brave smile, despite not feeling like they had.

'And the dwarves?' Azral said drowsily.

He was beginning to drift out of consciousness again, his eyelids becoming heavy.

'Don't you worry Azral. Everything is going to be just fine,' Grumpty said soothingly.

Azral smiled but didn't say anything and soon afterwards he had fallen asleep once more.

~~~

That night a celebration was held to honour the fallen. Tools were put down and restoration work left until the following day, or the day after depending on how hard the elves partied. The dwarves had observed curiously from the treeline, as elves danced around fires and joyful music filled the clearing.

It was odd to see such festivities after so much death and destruction, but in a way it made more sense to the Dwarf Queen than the broody mourning her people were famous for. It took some encouragement but eventually the dwarves were coaxed into joining the merry throng. Many clearly wanted to partake but seemed hesitant, as it wasn't traditional when honouring the dead.

The Dwarf Queen remedied this by saying to hell with tradition. She observed contentedly as the elves and dwarves mingled. It was an historic day. Not only would she soon have a new territory to occupy, but the long animosity and feud between elves and dwarves had been rectified.

The Dwarf Queen had never really felt a strong bond with the

Haggard Wolf. Their relationship had been based solely on profit, but with Grumpty she had found an ally that shared her passion for change.

~~~

The next few months saw some significant changes take place. Grumpty and Barkle had helped the Dwarf Queen locate a new area with the help of the owls in the sky. Azral, now fully recovered, Ogle and Nut had meanwhile overseen the rebuilding and redevelopment of the village. The original plan had been to restore the elven settlement to how it had been in the first place. But the dwarves had offered some suggestions to improve the structure and resilience of the new dwellings to be built.

By reinforcing the wooden frames with metal and iron it would make the huts stronger and less likely to be broken into or destroyed. Once again, they had sent the wolves away with their tails between their legs but after the carnage caused, the elves didn't want to leave it up to chance. In return for their help in the redesigns of the village, the elves assisted the dwarves in starting up a new settlement.

As per Grumpty and Barkle's suggestions they had settled on a place close to a river with good access to sunlight. As it was an area completely outside the Dwarf Queen's experience the elves had helped them at the beginning. The pay off between the two races grew more beneficial over time, and when they eventually began trading with one another, both communities started to thrive better than ever.

It wasn't just in terms of the settlements that change occurred. The two leaders that oversaw these transitions had also encountered change. Originally the Dwarf Queen was going to merely help the segment of dwarves, who were starting the new forest settlement. But over time she became more and more interested and invested in that, than life back in the mountains.

Much to everyone's surprise she stepped down as queen, passing the torch over to her young advisor. She was confident that the insightful dwarf would make a good leader and continue the important work she had started. Despite still feeling like she had work left to do, she had fallen in love with the forest and for once in her life she chose to follow her heart over her head.

Grumpty on the other hand had done the complete opposite. His plan was to serve as a temporary leader while the elves got back on their feet. But the passing of Mugleaf had made him realise that his connection with the village and the elves was stronger than he thought.

As much as he adored travelling the skies with the owls and exploring new lands, a part of him felt the need to be among his kin. Especially at a time when they needed a gentle but firm guiding hand.

Mother Owl had understood and told him that any time he needed a break he knew where to find her. Grumpty hoped more than anything, that peace would now ensue. Not only had they resolved the decades of long hostility with the dwarves, but they had also gained them as an ally.

As long as the wolves existed, he remained aware that there was always the possibility of more conflict. But with a stronger settlement and friends and allies close at hand, the wolves would certainly think twice before attacking again.

Printed in Great Britain
by Amazon

66577267R00075